Seven Magpies

A novel

by Fiona Valpy

ISBN: 978-1-84914-223-6

Published via www.completelynovel.com

For Carin, my sister.

One for sorrow
Two for joy
Three for a girl and
Four for a boy
Five for silver
Six for gold
Seven for a secret never to be told.
Eight's a wish and
Nine a kiss
Ten is a time of joyful bliss.

Traditional rhyme
(Anonymous)

Chapter 1

Time goes by, as Madonna observed in one of her more philosophical moments, so slowly.

Especially when it's two in the morning and the prospect of sleep has become as unlikely as the prospect of an affordable bottle of Château Pétrus.

I'm seriously starting to regret some of the music I've downloaded to my iPod, which is now running on a loop in my head. I wonder idly whether her Madge-esty suffers from insomnia. Possibly not, I reflect, what with the singing career to keep on the boil, that fabulous figure to maintain and assorted children to look after. Though maybe even she's been through a bit of a sleepless patch with the divorce and all. Men. And another wave of humiliation and revulsion washes over me as the thought of Roddy elbows its way to the top of my mind yet again.

Roddy and Camilla. The woman – girl really; inevitably she's some years younger than me – he's been having an affair with. For several months it turns out. And has now moved in with. Seamlessly, having packed his bags and moved out of my flat last week. Six days ago. And six lonely, sleepless nights, each of which has stretched itself out into a gaping chasm of minutes and seconds. The hours between two and four are the worst, when the hands of my alarm clock seem scarcely able to drag themselves round. Funny, though, how at the same time I can hear the ticking of my biological clock in the background racing faster and faster. It doesn't take an Einstein to work out the relativity of that one, as my body accelerates headlong towards sterility. Thirty-seven years old and counting...

Stop going round this loop. Think about something else. I need to get some sleep. My eyes feel gritty with weariness. If only I could stop the thoughts from fluttering and whirling in my head like a flock of noisy starlings that refuse to settle down for a quiet night's roosting.

Tomorrow is the trip to France. I mentally run through what I need to pack... passport, tickets, file of tasting notes and background information on the wine estates I'm going to visit, two business suits, five shirts, the black ankle boots...

A car alarm begins to sound a few streets away. Far enough that I don't need to do anything about it. But still close enough to bore into my brain like a dentist's drill into a sore tooth. Great, now I'm never going to get to sleep.

I glance at the clock. Ten past two. Time goes by... so slowly.

*

The difference between good wine and mediocre wine, I muse as I swing onto the autoroute, heading south away from dark grey English skies, travelling beneath the paler grey skies of Normandy towards the bright early-spring sunshine of the south, is the same as the difference between good sex and mediocre sex. To be good, it has to engage the mind as well as the senses.

No-one knows this better than the French. On the wine front at least. Probably on the sex front too, although I wouldn't know.

(Must remember to share this theory with my friend-and-fellow-buyer Annie when I get back, she'll appreciate it. And, knowing Annie, she may well be able to enlighten me further. On the sex front at least.)

French Wine is still one of the world's outstanding brands. Like Italian Shoes. Or Egyptian Cotton. Or Russian Caviar. It's one of those iconic commodities that's spawned a thousand wannabes, a benchmark against which all others are measured. Despite hot competition from New World wines, which has plunged the wine industry here into depression in recent years, in arguments with my colleagues I still maintain French supremacy to be the case.

"I love my job," I sing to myself. As a Buyer for Wainright's, an independent wine merchant's with a handful of shops dotted strategically on high streets in small towns across Sussex and Hampshire, I come to France a couple of times a year to visit producers and try any new wines that sound promising. I know it sounds quite a glamorous job, but the reality is a good deal more mundane. Most of my working hours are spent sitting behind my computer in the small dusty office above the shop in Arundel, dealing with product information and the somewhat tedious logistics of ordering. Once a month I visit each of the shops to keep staff up to date with the latest wine news and to help run tastings for clients. But a couple of times a year I hop across the Channel, spending a fortnight on the east side of France visiting Burgundy and the Rhône valley, and another fortnight in the west. This time I'm heading for the Loire and then on to Bordeaux. And the added bonus is that I've tacked on a few days' holiday at the end to stay with my favourite aunt.

Actually she's my only aunt, but Liz would be my favourite one even if I had others.

In fact you may have heard of her – Liz Chamberlain was something of a celebrity in the Swinging Sixties when she made a name for herself with her photography. Her iconic portraits of rock stars and artists are still re-printed from time to time, (especially, it has to be said, accompanying obituaries these days). But she moved to the depths of rural France in the early Seventies and completely turned her back on the glamour and buzz of her London life, becoming something of a recluse. She hasn't lost her eye for beauty, although she turned her camera lens from celebrities to the countryside surrounding her new home and picked up commissions to take photos for books on the wines of Bordeaux and the landscapes and wildlife of southern France. But now she's approaching seventy and her passion has waned with the advent of digital photography as, she says, the challenge and artistry have gone.

I can't wait to see her. A few days spent sitting in her beautiful garden is just the therapy I need right now. I know she'll ask me all about the break-up with Roddy and be outraged on my behalf. A good female solidarity session will give my battered self-esteem a much-needed boost and Liz's dry wit and easy warmth are always balm for a bruised soul.

I re-tune the radio to a French music station and feel my spirits lift a little. The flat, northern landscape rolls by and a sign announces that I'm entering Picardie.

The sledgehammer blow of Roddy's betrayal and departure was nothing in comparison with Dad's death last year, which was more like being hit by a wrecking-ball. But Roddy struck the still-open wound of my grief right on the spot and the heavy ache in my heart feels utterly unbearable at times. Talk about a double-whammy.

My father died much as he had lived, in a quiet, gentlemanly, considerate manner, falling silently to the ground in the back garden of my parents' home in West Sussex. A massive heart-attack, the doctors explained. Out of the blue. Nothing anyone could have done. My mother was her normal poised self when she phoned to tell me, and her cool, remote manner made me wonder, not for the first time, whether she had ever really loved my father. Sometimes it's hard to believe that she and Liz are sisters, the one so warm, funny and bohemian, living a rather hermit-like life tucked away in the depths of rural France, and the other such a reserved and proper Sussex matron, with a penchant for social Bridge and designer handbags.

We scattered his ashes at the edge of our garden, where our boundary gives on to neighbouring fields and the view southwards across the rolling slopes of the Downs, beside the bench where he used to come and sit to watch the sky turning from blue to rose to black on summer evenings, as swallows swooped and flitted overhead.

I blink to clear the pooling tears from my eyes and give myself a little shake mentally. Time to pull in at a service station for a croissant and a cup of hot, strong black coffee. After my sleepless night and early start this morning, I badly need a restorative boost of carbs and caffeine for the long drive ahead.

Chapter 2.

After a week's foraging in the Loire, notching up hundreds of miles in my selfless quest to seek out delicious bargains for the clients of Wainright's, I arrive in Blaye, the most northerly point of the Bordeaux region. Whilst the Loire Valley is a gracious and imposing region of France, with an air of refinement to both the area and its wines that is a source of quiet pride to its inhabitants, of the two regions that I'm visiting on this trip Bordeaux is my favourite.

The Loire has a dreamy quality to its elegant chateaux and their manicured grounds, but the Bordeaux region has a more gutsy, busy, purposeful feel. The Bordeaux winemaking area must be one of the biggest in the world and is certainly the best known. It is dissected by the broad rivers of the Dordogne and Garonne and turns its face bravely towards the Bay of Biscay, staring down some of its upstart New World cousins across the Atlantic Ocean. In the Médoc the best known – and frighteningly expensive – First Growth châteaux make their prestigious wines which sell the world over for several hundreds of whatever currency you happen to be in. Further east, the land rises into the *côteaux*, the clay-and-limestone ridges which dominate the valley floors, where you find St

Emilion and Pomerol, journey's end for many a wine pilgrim. But these famous names only tell half the story. The region is rich in *petits châteaux*, which are the engine-room of this powerhouse of world winemaking.

Harry Wainright still handles the buying "en primeur" from the *grands chateaux* for private clients, and each Wainright's shop stocks a few hallowed bottles of classic big-name wines like Lafite-Rothschild and Cos d'Estournel, mouth-watering wines at eye-watering prices. But my job here is, I think, far more interesting. I come to dig and delve in the less well-known corners of the Bordeaux region to seek out unknown, but still excellent, wines that we will sell in our shops at the sort of prices normal people pay. They are the wines that you'd buy to take to a dinner party, classy and sophisticated but readily drinkable without having to be buried in a cobweb-festooned cellar for a decade or so. Graves, Entre-Deux-Mers, Côtes de Blaye, Sainte Foy Bordeaux... some names are more familiar on the British high street than others.

Tonight I am staying in a fine old château which offers *chambres d'hôtes*. The owner, an elegant Frenchwoman, greets me warmly and shows me to my room. Tall shuttered windows look out across the parkland at the front of the house which is studded with magnificent chestnut trees, whose tender green leaves are just starting to unfurl. The room is as elegant as its owner. Its high corniced ceiling gives it an airiness, despite a plethora of heavy pieces of antique furniture, and the polished wooden floorboards and fine, yet worn, rugs are bathed in pools of golden light from the setting sun.

I unpack, hanging my suits and shirts in an imposing mahogany armoire, brush my teeth and spray on a little perfume to freshen up. I avoid wearing any during the day when I'm tasting, so the ritual of allowing myself a generous spritz of Jo Malone marks the transition from work to leisure time in my day.

Before I walk into the village for supper at the small restaurant there, (three delicious courses of French home-cooking plus half a *pichet* of house wine and there's still change from twenty Euros), I lie on the bed and read through my notes on the châteaux I'll be visiting in the next few days. Two are regular suppliers already, so these are really courtesy visits to maintain contact and ensure that the latest vintages are up to scratch. I'll also visit a handful of other *domaines* to research possible new lines. My mouth waters in anticipation of the juicy, fruity wines that I'll be tasting. After wall-to-wall whites in the Loire, I'm looking forward to sinking my teeth into some gutsy, full-bodied Clarets. With this in mind, I jot down a couple of ideas for possible inclusion in the tasting notes that I'll be compiling later.

Suddenly hungry, I pick up my handbag and jacket and hurry down the imposing staircase of the château, letting myself out of the heavy front door and closing it carefully behind me. As I stride briskly the few hundred yards along the small country road into the village, I am overcome with a longing to have my father here with me to share this evening meal.

It was with him that I learned to taste wine. He made his living as a wine-writer and became editor of 'Carafe' magazine, so wine was always a feature at the dinner table in our house, even in the 1970s when the odd bottle of Mateus Rosé or Blue Nun was the limit of most people's forays into this sophisticated and somewhat exclusive territory. From an early age he encouraged me to taste, in tiny quantities to be swirled around the mouth before spitting into a *crachoir*. Part of the delight in my childhood was to watch him send a perfectly-aimed stream of wine into the spittoon with a nonchalant elegance which completely belied the crudity of the action, elevating it to performance art.

He made me think about the different layers of flavours in each wine and encouraged me to describe what I could taste. "Don't be bashful," he'd say. "There's no right and wrong. It's a personal thing. Do you like it or not? If so, why? If not, why not?" He would bring a handful of small jars through from the spice rack in the kitchen and hold each one under my nose. "Think about what you can smell. That's cinnamon, remember it. And this one that smells like sweaty socks is cumin – you'll often find a whiff of it in some of the very best wines. Along with just a hint of horse manure." I would giggle at the thought of sweaty socks and horse manure and my mother would tut disapprovingly.

When I had applied for a job at Wainright's as a sales assistant, ("Get in on the shop floor, literally," said Dad, "it's the only way to learn if you're serious about getting into the wine trade."), probably the name had helped. "Gina Peplow, eh?" said Harry Wainright at my interview, peering sharply at me over his glasses. "Any relation to David?" But if a spot of nepotism had helped me get my first job, ever since then I had worked hard and earned my subsequent promotions to shop manager, buying assistant and finally Buyer in my own right. It's a tough and highly competitive world and I am well aware that there are many able candidates, at any given time, looking for a job like mine. Choosing the right wines to offer a balanced, interesting range that will keep attracting clients into Wainright's shops is absolutely critical. With the vast majority of people succumbing to the easy simplicity and in-your-face marketing of supermarket wines, (Buy two get one free! Reduced from £7.99!), the smaller independent wine merchants are having to fight hard to survive these days.

After the meal I pick my way back to the château somewhat gingerly. It's dark on the small country road, but it's a crisp, clear spring night and the moon and stars are out, so I can just make out the grass verge and follow it carefully. I open the big front door, (left unlocked, as is so often the custom in rural France), then creep on tiptoes up the creaking staircase to my room and the soft, warm embrace of the big feather bed. And, if I'm lucky, a full night's sleep.

*

I spend a happy week criss-crossing the area and unearthing some great new lines to add to the Wainright's range, ending up in the eastern-most corner of the region, where Liz's rambling stone farmhouse perches on the edge of the ridge above the broad valley of the Dordogne river.

The surrounding land, planted with neat rows of vines and plum orchards, was sold off long ago to local farmers. Liz bought just the house and its garden, a stretch of rough lawn bounded by tall oak trees. I turn into the lane between the vines and then up her dusty drive. It's been a long couple of weeks on the road and I bring the car thankfully to a halt in her courtyard, where pots of blue grape hyacinths and creamy narcissus are in bloom. Later, in the summer, she'll plant out the bright geraniums which I know will be clustered on every windowsill inside the house to keep them from the winter frosts.

Suddenly I realise how exhausted I am. It's not only the driving that's tiring, remembering to keep on the right side of the road. Speaking French non-stop takes its toll as well. I studied the language at school, where we were taught the literary language of Molière and Gide. After I started work for Wainright's I realised I needed to learn business French, another matter altogether, and I did some crash evening classes. I'm pretty good at the technicalities of winemaking too, but normal, everyday, conversational French is still hard work. I'll be chattering along fairly fluently and then suddenly an unknown phrase will loom up like a linguistic brick wall and I'll have to resort to miming or leafing through my pocket dictionary in a flurry of frustration. So it's something of a relief to be back in English-speaking territory now my busy fortnight is over.

As I clamber out of the car, the kitchen door opens and Liz emerges to greet me with arms outstretched. "Gina darling," she exclaims, "You look as though you need a good meal and an even better night's sleep. Fortunately you've come to the right place!" I hug my aunt warmly and am struck by a sudden feeling of frailty about her. She's always been slim, which goes with her quick, busy energy I suppose, but I haven't seen her for nearly a year and she's looking fragile and more bird-like than ever with her bright, sharp-eyed glance and neat cap of cropped white hair.

She ushers me into the kitchen. "Come and meet my lovely neighbour, Mireille. Madame Mireille Thibault, my niece Gina Peplow. I don't think you've met before." A tiny, very upright lady dressed in black stands to shake my hand, her face an etching of deep wrinkles which crease even further with her warm smile.

"Liz has told me a great deal about you," she says in French with just a slight twang of the south-western accent that is common around here.

"Mireille lives in the house just up the lane, on the other side," says Liz.

"Ah *oui*," I reply, "I know where you are. The new house, next to the big plum orchard?"

"*Oui, c'est moi*," she smiles. "And now I must be getting back. Two of my grandchildren will be arriving any minute and if I don't get there first they'll eat the whole of the cake I've made. They're always starving when they come out of school. Goodbye Mademoiselle, enjoy your stay with your aunt." She hugs Liz and disappears off up the drive.

"What a nice lady," I remark.

"Isn't she great?" says Liz. "So nice to have such a lovely friend and neighbour. I'm lucky she bought the new house. She lived closer to Sainte Foy before that and moved here about a year ago after her husband died. Now," she continues, holding me at arm's length to take a better look at me, "What's first? I think a shower and unpack and then a nice glass of something chilled and white? You look exhausted."

I go back out to the courtyard to bring my bag in from the car and as I re-enter the kitchen a large black cat appears to wind himself around my ankles. "Hello Lafite," I say, putting my bag down and bending to stroke his glossy coat. "You're looking extremely well." His deep purr reverberates and he butts his broad head lovingly against my hand.

My aunt found a cat and two small kittens in her woodshed one early summer's day about a dozen years ago. No-one round about had any idea where they came from, although they weren't wild so Liz suspected they'd just been dumped by someone upon the unwelcome arrival of the two new additions. So she adopted them, naming the mother Margaux and the two kittens Latour and Lafite. Sadly Latour came to an early end when he ate some poison put down by a local farmer to kill foxes, but Margaux lived to a ripe old age and her remaining son is still going strong. "How old is Lafite now?" I ask.

"He'll be fourteen in a couple of months' time. He's getting rather staid these days. Not nearly as good a mouser as he once was – he doesn't exactly earn his keep. Spends most of the time lying by the fire or on his chair in my bedroom. Still, he's good company."

"And no doubt just as utterly pampered and adored as ever," I smile.

Liz shows me to the guest bedroom. Not that I need to be shown the way, it's thoroughly familiar from my many stays with her over the years. In my teens I started coming here on my own for a week or two during the long summer holidays. First, Mum, Dad and I would have our family fortnight in

Salcombe in July. My mother would lounge elegantly on the beach behind a large pair of sunglasses and the latest copy of Tatler or Homes and Gardens, while Dad and I made sandcastles or, when I was old enough, sailed a small dinghy upriver, away from the frenetic bustle of boats in the harbour to explore the creeks hidden behind sloping shoulders of green farmland. He'd always bring a pair of binoculars for bird-spotting. Once we saw a kingfisher, the colour and speed of an electric shock, darting down from a dead branch overhanging the water. And another time we sat together on the bank, entranced by the bizarre movements of a dipper, one of the shyest of birds, as it bobbed and bowed on a rock before walking right into the water, foraging beneath the surface in search of food.

Then, with August still stretching before me, I'd be put on a plane and met at Bordeaux airport by Liz. My mother never seemed keen to come along – too much to do in the garden after being away in Devon, and she'd miss her Bridge, she always said – and I was secretly pleased. My holidays with Liz were always wonderful, sun-filled, fascinating weeks of freedom, helping her in her gloriously wild garden or visiting the local markets to pick out colourful fresh produce. We'd bring the food back so that she could teach me to cook classic French dishes. She'd always choose a local wine to go with what we'd made, helping me to understand how the right wine complements and enhances even the simplest meal. "The most expensive bottle isn't necessarily the best," she'd say, twisting the corkscrew and levering out the cork with a satisfying pop. "It depends entirely on what you're eating. Let's try this red from Castillon with the steaks tonight – you'll see how its gutsiness is perfect with the chewy meat and the garlic butter."

I am pleased to see that nothing in the spare room has been changed. The whitewashed walls are hung with framed photos of the local landscape – Liz's work of course. I know and love each one: the stick-like vines on the *côteau* plunging into mist lying in the river valley below which is rosy pink in winter sunshine; the white clouds of blossom in the plum orchards in spring; a golden willow perfectly reflected in hazy autumn light on the Dordogne. There are rag rugs on the terracotta-tiled floor and a pretty *toile de jouy* quilted spread on the double bed. I used to think it was the height of sophistication when I was younger, to sleep in such a big bed, quite unlike the modest single one in my bedroom at home. There's a pretty jug of spring flowers on the bedside table, along with a small pile of paperbacks. Liz is an avid reader and I know she'll have put these to one side for me thinking I would enjoy them too. "What bliss to be here," I sigh, turning to hug my aunt.

"Get yourself settled in and come through when you're ready," she says and kisses my forehead gently in return.

*

When I come through to the kitchen half an hour later a delicious smell greets me and Liz, pushing a casserole back into the oven, straightens up from shutting the door. "Coq au vin", she says. "Hope that's ok." She knows it's one of my favourites. Her recipe is the perfect comfort food, the syrupy juices suffused with earthy flavours of wild mushrooms and fragrant thyme. "Now," she turns to the fridge, "where's that bottle of wine?" She brings out a bottle with the typical rounded shoulders of the Bordeaux appellation. "Thought we'd have a little Graves – I hope you're not sick to death of it after this past week?"

"Not a bit. Any variation on a theme of Sauvignon Blanc is fine by me."

"Shall we take our glasses out to the terrace?" suggests Liz. "The sun's just going down but let's catch the last half hour."

The terrace is on the west of the house, the other side from the courtyard. Even though it's still only early March, there's warmth in the suntrap of its stone paving against the wall of the house. We sit on the bench facing the setting sun.

A magpie flutters down from the branches of an oak tree onto the grass, almost immediately followed by a second one. "Two for joy," I say, smiling. "Very apt at this precise moment. You taught me that rhyme. And also to say 'Hello Mr Magpie, how's your lovely wife today?' when you only see one, to try and keep the bad luck away, do you remember? I still say it in my head even now."

Liz smiles. "I know. Not that we're superstitious or anything. But, oh dear, I don't think it's been working very well for you just recently has it? What's all this about Roddy?" I tell her briefly what's happened and she is, as I knew she would be, comfortingly outraged on my behalf.

"That complete bastard," she says, making me smile at the incongruous language from such a genteel old lady.

"Aunt Elizabeth, really!" I tease.

"Well, what a spineless shit, carrying on behind your back like that. I hate to say it, but I didn't really take to him that time you brought him here last year. Too smooth for his own good. And not nearly good enough for you, if you ask me. Although, of course, you didn't and I'd never have dreamt of saying so at the time. And who's called Roderick these days anyway," she continues, warming to her theme. "Like something out of PG Wodehouse!"

"I know," I sigh. "He was named after a bachelor uncle in the hope that he'd inherit some huge family pile. The funny thing is, though, the old bloke ended up marrying some glamorous divorcée at the eleventh hour. She had three children and he left the whole lot to them instead. So Roddy ended up with nothing but the name."

"Well it serves him right in that case," retorts Liz, still briskly indignant. "I've never heard such nonsense." She pauses. Then says, a little more gently, "Did you really love him?"

I hesitate, contemplating how to answer her question. "I don't know if it was love exactly, but I'd become very used to having him around. It certainly wasn't a grand passion, but at my age you can't afford to hang around waiting for the love of your life to come along, you know. I did think we were probably going to get married eventually..." I tail off, hearing how half-hearted this sounds.

And I try not to think about the difference between good wine and mediocre wine. But it suddenly strikes me that Roddy was more of a bottle of plonk than a Grand Cru. More plonker than prince now I come to think about it.

"Well you deserve far better than that," retorts Liz briskly. "The love of your life is exactly what you should be waiting for. Don't settle for anything less."

"But what if the right man doesn't come along? What if I never have children? I always imagined I would, but that clock's running down fast. What if I don't meet anyone in time?"

"Then you will live a happy and fulfilled life on your own," Liz says firmly. "It's not that bad, you know."

"Is that what you did? Decide not to settle for anything less than the man of your dreams, I mean? Did he just never come along?"

Liz reaches down to deadhead some daffodils growing in a pot beside us. "Oh, I met the man of my dreams alright. But it was complicated. In fact so complicated that it was impossible. And yes, after that I did decide that I could never settle for second best. But that's way back in prehistoric times now." From her brisk change of tone I know she is firmly fending off any further questions. "It's far too late for an old dinosaur like me. But you are a mere spring chicken, with everything going for you and time still on your side, so just hang on in there. I know the right man for you will come along. And you have your career as well of course. How long have you been at Wainright's now? Must be getting on for twenty years isn't it? Do you think you might want to make a move at some stage?"

"I don't know." I frown and take another sip of my wine. "I love the company and I love what I do, and I was perfectly happy to keep jogging along until recently. I suppose because I thought Roddy and I would be starting a family before too long. Under those circumstances I'd have been content just ticking over at work. Easier to balance the whole motherhood thing too. But now all that's changed of course."

"Ah, the eternal compromise of the working mother," says Liz sagely. "In my day you had to choose, but these days I thought you could have it all – the fulfilling career and the clutch of perfect children too."

"Hm, I suspect the reality is still a little trickier to achieve, whatever it may look like on the pages of the glossy magazines. Anyway, I now appear to have neither."

"Well there's nothing to stop you applying for other jobs, is there?" says Liz. "Any prospect of a promotion at Wainright's?"

"Only if Harry throws in the towel. As a France specialist I'd need to go for his job. Or sell my soul and go over to the dark side. New World wines," I explain as Liz looks at me quizzically. "No, I'd have to look elsewhere to stay with French wines, and there are fewer of those jobs about these days. The New World is where the growth is now. Although the whole sector is battling a bit in the current climate. Sales are down across the board."

"Well I'm pleased to hear you're remaining loyal to your roots," says Liz with a nod of approval.

I'm starting to feel considerably better as a result of my darling aunt's company, the gentle glow of the evening sunshine and the deliciously crisp, cool wine. I breathe in a deep breath and let it right out, feeling my tense shoulders relax a little for the first time in weeks. The air is suddenly cool and Liz shivers a little on the bench beside me. "Come on," I say, offering her my arm, "Let's go in. That coq au vin smells better than ever."

*

That night I sleep. And oh, the relief to wake up in the morning and see the hands of my watch standing at half past seven rather than two or three. I didn't shut my shutters when I went to bed, and the morning light is already streaming in at the window, casting the fat buds on the wisteria branches that hang outside into elongated, dancing shadows across the bedspread. I stretch, luxuriating in the knowledge of a good night's sleep behind me and a sunny day ahead. I can already hear Liz in the kitchen, talking to Lafite as she puts food into his bowl. There's no great hurry to get up and I look through the books beside my bed, select one from the pile and read for a while. Lafite, his breakfast devoured, shoulders open the door of my room with an inquisitive chirrup and jumps onto the bed, settling down companionably beside me.

Once I'm finally up and dressed, I find Liz in her study. The book-lined room, with its tall, large-paned windows looking out onto the courtyard, is usually a comfortable muddle of papers, magazines and folders full of old photographs, negatives and contact sheets. Today it's messier than ever, positively awash with heaps of paper in a kaleidoscope of colours and forms and in the middle of it all sits Liz, glasses perched on the end of her nose, peering at a folder of photos. I wade through the detritus and bend down to kiss her soft, wrinkled cheek. She looks up with a slight start. "Sorry, didn't see you there. I was back in the Sixties with Keith and Ron." She holds up a black and white print of the Rolling Stones grinning into the camera, fresh-faced images of their current-day selves. "I'm having a bit of a clear out," she explains with a sweep of her hand. "Time I got rid of some of this nonsense. Which reminds me," she continues, "come upstairs to my room. I've got a few things I thought you might quite like."

Liz's bedroom takes up the entire attic of the long, low farmhouse. She converted it to living space when she moved in, adding low windows beneath the eaves and skylights to let in the sun. The clear out obviously extends to her wardrobe as well as her study, as piles of clothes are heaped on the floor and every chair around the room. On the bed, next to a roll of black bin bags, there's a small pile, neatly folded. Liz picks up the top item and shakes it out, holding it up against herself. It's a top made of floating layers of creamy silk with long, softly flared sleeves and a plunging neckline.

"Wow, that's gorgeous!" I exclaim.

Liz hands it to me. "Try it on and see if it fits. I thought it would suit you. It's an early Ossie Clark piece. Have a look through these others as well, see if there's anything else there you'd like. Here, take them to your room," she says, putting the pile of rainbow-coloured fabrics into my arms and draping the cream tunic across the top. "You can try them on while I get your breakfast. Oh, and I meant to tell you, we're invited to Hugh and Celia Everett's for drinks this evening. You don't have to come if you don't want to, but they said you'd be most welcome."

"I'd love to come," I reply. "I'm very fond of them both."

The Everetts are old family friends. Celia was at school with my mother and my aunt and she was Head Girl when Liz was a hippy rebel, according to my mother. Three years younger than the pair of them, Mum worshipped them both from the lowly ranks of the Upper Fourth. Despite their divergent styles, Liz and Celia have remained friends and, having holidayed in the region for years, on Hugh's retirement from the Diplomatic Service, the Everetts bought a house a few miles from Liz and set about establishing themselves as lynch pins of the local social scene.

"Well, there's sure to be a crowd there. Celia always invites the world and his wife. Perhaps there'll be an eligible bachelor who we can team you up with," she adds with an arch twinkle.

*

As we arrive at the Everetts', Hugh throws open the door of their rather grand home on the outskirts of the picturesque village of Gensac and warmly embraces Liz, then turns to kiss me on both cheeks. "Goodness me," he says chivalrously, "Gina you just get more and more beautiful."

Tonight I feel beautiful, because I'm wearing the vintage top Liz gave me. The minute I put it on its clever, flattering cut draped softly and sexily over

29

my figure, my complexion glowing against its soft colour. When I looked at my reflexion in the age-spotted wardrobe mirror in my room I'd felt a sudden boost to my battered self-confidence.

Hugh ushers us ahead of him into a large, high-ceilinged room full of chattering, laughing people and Celia detaches herself from a group near the door, coming over to hug us warmly. "Liz darling, and Gina too, how wonderful. Grab a drink," she says pouring us each a glass of wine from a bottle on the table behind her, "and come and mingle. Liz, you know everyone I think. Gina, come with me, I simply must introduce you to Nigel." She takes me by the hand and leads me through the throng of guests to a trio standing beside one of the windows. "Gina Peplow, meet Sally and Oliver McKay and Nigel Yates."

With bright smiles of something that looks suspiciously like relief, Sally and Oliver turn towards me. They've clearly been pinned down for some time by Nigel, whose pink shiny shirt matches his equally pink shiny face which is topped off with what seems to be the beginnings of a comb-over. My heart sinks as Sally and Oliver, seizing the opportunity to make a break for it, mutter something about getting another drink and edge away towards the table, brutally leaving me stuck in their place. I look round for Celia, but she's already sailed off to oil the social wheels of her party elsewhere, and I catch a glimpse of Liz across the room. She's grinning at me wickedly and raises her glass with a flourish that confirms what I already suspected: it's a set-up.

Sighing inwardly, I turn politely to Nigel, who is enthusiastically explaining that he's new in town and asking if I live nearby. He's recently bought a wreck of a house here and is in the throes of major renovations which he describes with gusto - and many complaints about the shortcomings of French workmen and the difficulties in finding decent plumbing fixtures – for the next half hour.

As he embarks on a detailed description of the installation of his new septic tank (with far too much information about solids, liquids and something called a leaching field) I allow my gaze to wander. Liz is deep in conversation with Hugh, who leans in close to listen to something she's saying, then throws his head back to roar with laughter. I wonder idly whether perhaps he's the mystery man that she loved – they share the same wicked sense of humour and he's clearly always been very fond of her. Watching them together though, I realise they are 'just good friends', in the non-euphemistic sense of the phrase. It's far more likely that Liz's unattainable lover was a rock star (Mick or Ron?) or perhaps even royalty...

Suddenly I realise that Nigel's fascinating description of selected plumbing highlights has paused and he is looking at me as if expecting an answer to something he has just asked. Blushing, I say, "I'm sorry, I didn't quite catch what you said there – terribly difficult to hear with all this chat." I gesture with my glass in a vague sweep that takes in the assembled throng.

"I just wondered whether you'd like to pop round and see the house sometime? I could show you what I've done so far."

Tempting though the thought of a guided tour of Nigel's septic tank may be, I am relieved to have the cast-iron excuse of my departure for home in thirty-six hours time. Nigel looks momentarily crestfallen, but then brightens saying, "Never mind, we'll organise something next time you're over. There'll be even more to show you by then I expect."

Thankfully, Liz materialises at his shoulder, introducing herself and then saying with a smile, "I'm sorry to have to tear Gina away, but there's someone I must introduce her to. So nice to have met you." And she firmly takes my arm, leaving Nigel turning to a group to one side of us who look as if they may need enlightening on the ins and outs (as it were) of modern sanitation systems in old French houses.

"You looked as if you needed saving," Liz says to me with a grin once we're safely out of earshot. ""What on earth was Celia thinking? She said she had a nice eligible man lined up for you."

"Yes, I rather guessed the two of you had hatched that particular plot," I reply laughing, "but next time, please don't go to any trouble on my behalf."

"Oh dear, this isn't exactly the richest of hunting grounds, I'm afraid," says Liz. "Now, do you want another glass of wine or shall we bow out graciously and get home for supper?"

"Well, unless you and Celia have another hot date lined up for me, I think a cheese omelette and a good book sound like bliss."

*

The next day is my last full day in France before I drive north on Sunday to catch the overnight ferry home, going straight in to the office on Monday morning. Saturday is market day in Sainte Foy La Grande and we spend a happy couple of hours browsing amongst the stalls of cheeses, oysters, spices and pyramids of fresh, colourful fruit and vegetables. We manage to find a free table at the cafe in the corner of the square and sink thankfully into two chairs, Liz's large wicker basket, overflowing with fresh produce and neat greaseproof paper-wrapped parcels, at our feet. As I blow onto the creamy surface of my *grand crème*, a familiar pink face appears through the crowd, waving enthusiastically.

"Aha, I've tracked you down," crows Nigel. "I thought you two lovely ladies might be here this morning." He looks around for a chair to pull up to our table but, luckily for us, there are none free on the crowded pavement in front of the cafe. Unabashed, with a flourish he pulls a small card out of his shirt pocket. "Thought I'd let you have my contact details. Let me know next time you're coming over and we'll get something in the diary. I can show you over the house, give you some lunch or whatever." Politely, and concentrating hard on avoiding catching Liz's eye, I take the card.

"Thanks," I say lamely. "That's a really kind thought."

"Well, must be going," says Nigel. "My bathroom tiles aren't going to grout themselves." I agree that this does indeed sound unlikely, and we shake hands. "*Au revoir* and *à bientôt* then, as we say here," he beams and disappears off through the crowd.

"Well," says Liz, "You certainly seem to have made an impression there!"

"Hmm, yes. The fact that there isn't another available Anglo-Saxon female under the age of sixty for about five hundred miles has nothing to do with it of course."

"Nonsense, don't put yourself down. Although come to think of it, it was probably the Ossie Clark top that did it," grins Liz. "Now come on, let's get home and get this food put away."

*

After lunch I drag a pair of battered sun-loungers out of the woodshed and set them up on the terrace, dusting off their winter wrapping of sticky strands of spiders' web. We sit side by side, lifting our faces to the sun, Liz with the local newspaper, *Sud-Ouest*, and me with my book. After a while I rest the book on my stomach, closing my eyes for just a minute...

I wake with a start some time later and swivel the watch on my wrist to squint at the time, noticing with pleasure that the strap has now made a faint white stripe against the pale gold of my skin after a day or two of French sun. It's nearly four o'clock and the sun-lounger next to me is deserted. I ease myself up stiffly, straightening my creased t-shirt, my mouth sticky with the staleness of the deep sleep of afternoon. Going into the house, I find Liz back in her study, sifting through papers on her lap.

"Cup of tea?" I ask.

"Lovely," she replies vaguely, deep in some old letters. She perches her glasses on top of her head and looks up with a smile. "You were out for the count."

"I know. Fresh air and good food are so exhausting."

I put the tea things on a tin tray and carry them through to the study, where Liz reaches to clear a space on a small table, piling folders onto the floor.

"You're inspiring me to have a good spring clean when I get home," I say. "I still haven't quite got round to carrying out my New Year's resolution of de-cluttering both my wardrobe and the flat. Minimalist chic will be my new watchword." I hand Liz a pretty bone china cup and saucer. "Earl Grey, no milk, that right?"

"Perfect," she smiles. "Minimalist chic, eh? Not sure that's really your style. Chic yes, minimalist no. And anyway, that's two watchwords."

I turn to pour my own cup of tea, settling myself in a sagging armchair, and am distracted by a pile of Vogue magazines from the late Sixties. Reaching for one I say, "Maybe I can find some inspiration here. That top you gave me could be the start of a whole new image. What do you think?" I leaf through the magazine, but there's no reply from Liz.

Glancing up, I notice that my aunt is sitting with her gaze fixed on the air in front of her. "Liz?" I say and then again more sharply, "Liz!" I jump to my feet as, still with a fixed gaze, she tilts slightly to one side and then teacup and saucer fall clattering to the floor at her feet, splattering papers and photographs with hot tea. I grab her arm and kneel down in front of her, shaking her shoulder and looking up into the fixed, faraway mask of her face. Slowly her eyes focus on mine and expression returns, a flicker of fear mirroring the terror that must be written on my face, before she gives a little start and tries to draw herself up to sit straight again in her chair.

"Oh dear," she says faintly. "Don't know what came over me there. Such a silly thing to do. Look what a mess I've made."

"Never mind that, I'll clean it up. But are you OK? What happened, did you feel faint?"

"I just blacked out for a second I think. Must have got a bit too much sun earlier."

She tries to stand and sways dizzily. I help her to her feet, am arm round her shoulders, which feel fragile and bony through the thin cotton of her blouse.

"Come on, let's get you upstairs. You'd better have a bit of a lie down."

In her room I settle her on her bed, slipping off her shoes and easing her feet, lumpy with bunions, onto the coverlet. I sit on the bed beside her, holding her hand.

"Look at you," she smiles, a little shakily. "I've frightened the living daylights out of you. Don't worry, it's just one of my turns. Part of the joys of old age."

"Do you have these 'turns' often then?" I ask.

"I've had one or two lately, but they soon pass. Must be low blood sugar or something. Nothing to make a fuss about." She yawns deeply. "Oh, I am sleepy though." She closes her eyes.

I stay with her, stroking the thin, age-spotted skin on the back of her hand as she drifts asleep.

Looking round her room, I take in the framed photos which have hung on these walls for as long as I can remember. They're all of birds – the bright eye, curved beak and exotic crest of a hoopoe; a grey heron tip-toeing on stick-like legs through a reed-bed in the river; a black and white print of a long 'v' of grey cranes which fly north at this time of year, looking and sounding like creaky barn doors with their vast wingspans and rusty, honking cries.

Listening to her faint but regular breathing, my eye falls on a picture in a heavy silver frame on her bedside cabinet. I don't remember seeing this one before. It's another black and white photo and I recognise the outline of a cedar tree which stands beside the drive. On it, at the ends of six of its branches, are perched three pairs of magpies, their black and white plumage sitting within the symmetry of the tree, rather like neatly-placed decorations on a Christmas tree. 'Six for gold,' I think to myself with a smile. 'In a frame of silver.' Trust Liz to see the beauty in the moment and be able to catch it on camera. It must appeal to her quirky sense of humour to have it sitting here beside her bed.

Lafite comes through the door on silent paws and jumps smoothly onto a chair on the other side of the bed. He settles down and watches us, eyes narrowed, and I feel reassured by his presence.

Checking again that Liz's breathing is quiet and regular, I leave her under the watchful gaze of the black cat and creep out of the room to go and clear up the spilt tea in the study.

*

Later, I tap on her bedroom door to ask if she'd like me to bring her supper up on a tray. She's awake, lying on her side and gazing at the photo of the magpies beside her. She turns and smiles. "Some scrambled eggs would be lovely, thanks. I'm feeling fine now. I think I'll come down. Give me a hand?"

As we sit over our supper at the kitchen table I say, "I'm worried about leaving you tomorrow. I really think you should go and see a doctor about these blackouts. Will you promise me you'll phone first thing on Monday morning? You should see your GP and you might need to be referred to a specialist."

"I'll be fine," says Liz. "I'll call Mireille if I start feeling funny again. She's a minute up the lane if I need her. In any case, she looks in every day to say hello when she knows I don't have anyone here. So don't worry, she's keeping an eye on me. And I'm honestly feeling OK now."

"Yes, but promise me you'll go and see the doctor," I insist.

"You young things are very bossy nowadays," she laughs, shaking her head, and I'm relieved to hear a little of the usual spark back in her voice.

"And some slightly less-young things are very stubborn," I retort. "Promise me."

"OK, OK," she holds up her hands in mock-surrender. "I promise."

Chapter 3.

Monday morning, and I shoulder open the door of the shop, a carton of six sample bottles of wine in my arms with my handbag and a large folder of notes from my trip balanced precariously on top of it.

"Hi Gina, good trip?" asks Sam, the shop manager, brightly as he dusts bottles before arranging them in a display beside the counter. "You're looking well. You've caught some sun."

He holds open the door for me and I make my way upstairs to the office, thankfully depositing wine, folder and bag onto my desk beside a pile of mail that's accumulated there over the time I've been away. That's the trouble with buying trips. They're wonderful while they last but you come back to piles of work to catch up with and no sympathy at all from colleagues who've been left behind grafting away while you've been off on what they see as a bit of a jolly.

Harry Wainright comes out of his corner office and peers at me over the top of his horn-rimmed glasses. "Ah Gina, there you are," he beams. "Good to have you back. What's this you've found?"

I open the box and show him the range of blended reds, whites and a deep rosé known in Bordeaux as a Clairet, from a small château to the south of St Emilion. "Very promising," he says, examining the labels. "Add them to the other samples in the tasting room. We'll include them in the blind tasting on Thursday evening."

The office door bangs open and Annie crashes into the room, breathless and laughing at some exchange she's just had with the staff in the shop. She's the buyer for New World wines and is as voluptuous, brash, loud and warm-hearted as many of the wines in her portfolio. "Hooray, Gina you're back! Looking forward to hearing all about it. Time for a drink after work tonight? I need to tell you all about the most gorgeous man I've just met."

"Like the hair," I say. Annie changes her hair colour about as often as she changes her men. Which is very often. When I left a fortnight ago she was a redhead. She's now a dramatically dark brunette. But with Annie Mackenzie, one always senses that blondeness is never far away.

I settle myself down at my desk and turn on my computer, sorting the pile of mail as it starts up. I groan inwardly when I get into my emails – 'You have 279 unread messages', the program helpfully tells me. The little red light on my phone is winking cheerily at me too, signifying yet more messages awaiting me on my voicemail, and I know I'll be lucky if there's time to dash out at lunchtime to grab a sandwich and bring it back to eat at my desk while I carry on ploughing my way through this lot. As well, *c'est la vie*.

Annie reappears at my elbow and places a mug of coffee between the piles of papers on my desk. "You'll be needing this," she grins, and heads back to her desk, leaving me to it.

I deal with my phone messages first, then turn to my emails. A few can be weeded out straight away, like the one from Nigeria beginning 'Dear Esteemed Partner, I have been given your name by a mutual friend as someone who is trustworthy...' and ending '... in order to receive your share of my $1,000,000 windfall simply send me your full bank details.' Or the ones that have slipped through the anti-spam net, offering me penis extensions and weight-loss wonder drugs.

As I page down I notice one from Roddy, (subject: Hello), which I studiously ignore until I have diligently worked through all the other messages.

It's well after six o'clock when, massaging my aching neck, I finally double-click on Roddy's name and read his email.

It's dated a week ago and says 'Just wondering how you're doing. Hope you're OK. Have been thinking about you. Give me a call sometime. R.'

I click the message shut, then sit staring at the computer screen for a few seconds before re-opening the email to scan it again. It's non-committal, but a definite invitation to re-open lines of contact. Hah, maybe he's realised what he's missing now his 'bit on the side' has moved to a more central – and no doubt less exciting – position. Or perhaps he's broken it off with her and I imagine a highly satisfactory scene where we meet up and he's contrite, begging me to take him back. Naturally, being strong-minded and highly-principled, I turn him down. But then after a suitable period of begging and a campaign involving several large bouquets of flowers, he convinces me that he has truly seen the error of his ways and will be faithful to me for ever more, I take him back, forgiving him in a mature and dignified manner. Perhaps even a diamond ring features at this point...

I snap myself out of my reverie with a shake of my head. "Yeah, and watch out for flying pigs too," I mutter under my breath.

"Sorry Gina, I didn't quite catch that?" asks Harry, on his way out of the office, briefcase in hand.

"Oh, good night Harry. Nothing, just talking to myself," I laugh.

"In that case, it's definitely time to get yourself home," he replies.

"Yup, I'm on my way. Just finishing up here." I take one more look at Roddy's message on the screen in front of me before briskly clicking 'delete' and shutting down the computer.

I glance at my watch as Annie and I make our way downstairs. This had better just be a quick drink. Must remember to call Liz when I get home and check that she's alright. And I'd better ring my mother too, to let her know I'm back safely and tell her about my trip.

*

The call comes about a fortnight later, and as my mother tells me the news of Liz's death I realise I knew this was coming but was studiously ignoring it. Like a small child who puts their hands over their eyes believing that if they can't see the monster, the monster can't see them.

I sit at my kitchen table, frozen in shock and grief, my Saturday morning shopping list in front of me. Bread, it says. Eggs, milk, washing-up liquid. The words seem to burn themselves into my dry eyes, mundane, meaningless, irrelevant. My mother's voice is calm and composed and for a moment I think I've fallen through a hole in time and am listening to her telling me of my father's death a year ago. But I force myself to listen to the words she's saying and they're different.

"A neighbour found her yesterday afternoon. A stroke they think, very sudden. Celia Everett called to tell me. She and Hugh are being wonderful, getting everything organised at that end, which is a huge help as their French is so good and they're on the spot. The funeral should be towards the end of the week. Apparently Liz left instructions."

My throat and chest feel constricted with the crushing pain of grief and loss. It hurts to speak.

"She knew it was coming," I say dully, a sudden vision of Liz in her study surrounded by piles of papers flashes into my mind. And then I remember the heaps of clothes in her room, and the roll of black bin bags. And I think of the Ossie Clark top she gave me, now hanging carefully in my wardrobe, and a sob escapes me like an air-bubble rising up from the deep ocean floor.

"Oh darling," says my mother. "I know how much she meant to you. Stay where you are, I'm coming over."

I place the phone on the table in front of me and its outline swims as my tears fall, blurring the ink on the shopping list beside it. I'm still sitting there, numb and shivering, when my mother rings the doorbell half an hour later.

The world is a colder place without my aunt in it.

*

The cremation is arranged for Friday afternoon. Mum and I are met at Bergerac airport the evening before by Hugh Everett and he whisks us back to Gensac. "Of course you'll stay with us," Celia had insisted during one of the many phone calls she and my mother have exchanged over the course of the week. I would have far preferred to stay in Liz's house, but that idea was swept briskly aside by the formidable organisational taskforce (Sussex and Gironde branches) that have taken charge of matters.

We sit in beautifully upholstered (Sanderson chintz) armchairs in the Everetts' beautifully decorated (Farrow and Ball) sitting room, sipping gin and tonics out of beautifully sparkling (Edinburgh crystal) glasses. Celia clasps a hand to her own beautifully upholstered (cashmere and pearls) bosom and sighs deeply. "Such a shock for us all, and a terrible loss. And especially hard for you Gina, we know how close you were to Liz and how fond she was of you." She pauses and looks across at Hugh, who has just sat down on the sofa beside Mum and is taking a long and thankful draught of his drink. "Darling," she prompts, "I think you have something to tell Gina?"

"Yes indeed," Hugh turns to me. "Liz had everything extremely well organised. A while ago she asked me to be an executor of her will, and I'm pleased to tell you Gina that she has left her entire estate to you. Not that it amounts to that much – it's really just the house and its contents. She had a little money invested to give her an annuity, and her state pension of course. And there's the occasional royalty from her books and photos, but that's just a trickle these days. The house is worth a bob or two though if you want to sell. Needs a bit doing to it, of course, but around here you can usually find an ex-pat looking for a project to take on."

This is moving too fast for me to take in. My immediate reaction is 'no way am I selling Liz's house', but then I pull myself up short. "But Mum, shouldn't some of this come to you?" I ask.

"Oh darling, that's so sweet of you, but no. I really don't need more than I have. Your father left me very comfortably provided for as you know. Of course Liz wanted you to have this, and quite right too. Just think what it would mean if you sold the house. You could use the money to pay off the mortgage on your flat, or to move up the property ladder and invest in something a little more desirable. It's a lovely opportunity."

My aunt's dead body is lying in a funeral home a few miles away and we are sitting here talking about selling her house and it being a 'lovely opportunity'. A wave of anger and disgust washes over me. I clutch my cold glass tightly to stop my hands from shaking and the ice cubes clink – an incongruously light-hearted sound.

Celia may be sharp and sometimes overbearing, but she's also kindly and perspicacious and she sees how wretched I'm feeling, my face reddening and my eyes filling with angry tears. "Well now," she says, patting my arm, "there's more than enough time for you to think things over. You don't have to take any decisions in a hurry and anyway it'll take a while for the notary to sort out all the paperwork. Let it sink in for a while. We'll keep popping in to check the house now and then, and of course Madame Thibault keeps an eye on the place. She's taken Lafite in you know. Apparently he was sitting beside Liz's body when Mireille Thibault found her, as if he was watching over her until help arrived. It was really very touching."

In a daze of emotional exhaustion I choke down supper and then take myself off to bed. Despite all the little comforting touches Celia has provided – a vase of fresh flowers, a bottle of drinking water, some relaxing bath oil - I feel empty and un-comforted. Lying under the quilted coverlet in the Everetts' second spare room (my mother is down the hall in the main guest suite), I spend a sleepless night, wishing I was in Liz's spare room - my spare room now - so that I could feel closer to her on this last night her body is on the Earth.

*

The crematorium is as drab and depressing as these places are the world over. Liz left very specific instructions and Hugh and Celia have arranged everything accordingly. The coffin is the plainest pine, but I place an armful of scented white lilies on it, my farewell gift to my aunt.

When we enter the small room where the service is to be conducted, my eyes swim as I make out a crowded blur of faces. Despite Liz's directive that her funeral was to be small, with no fuss, she couldn't deter the many friends, both French and English, who have turned up to see her off. Standing by the door is a familiar figure who earnestly pumps my hand. My mother raises a quizzical eyebrow and I make the introductions. "Nigel Yates, my mother Catherine Peplow." I finally manage to extricate myself from Nigel's sympathetic stream of platitudes, (lovely lady your aunt, greatly missed by one and all...) and catch sight of Mireille Thibault waiting patiently to one side. She puts her arms round me in a warm embrace, saying nothing, and for the first time since hearing the news of Liz's death I feel comforted. Overwhelmed, I stay in the circle of her arms for a minute until, patting my back gently she pulls back and her bright, wise old eyes look into mine. "You'll be coming to the house this weekend?" she asks. "Come and knock on my door. Lafite will be pleased to see you."

"Are you coming back to the Everetts' after the service?" I say. "They're having a reception and you'll be most welcome."

"Thank you but no. I'm just going to say my *adieus* to Liz here and then go home. But I'll see you tomorrow. *Bon courage* my dear."

And courage is exactly what I need half an hour later, as the coffin slides silently through the curtain and my aunt is gone.

*

Celia and my mother drop me at the end of the lane the next morning and drive off down the hill to the bustle of the market, and no doubt a lingering gossip over a coffee in the square.

It's a beautiful morning and I walk up the lane between the neat vines which are beginning to weave themselves into a lush tapestry along their supporting wires. Pink and purple orchids nestle in the long grass beside the verge and the musical chatter of birdsong floats on the soft breeze.

I walk past the end of Liz's driveway and continue as far as Mireille's neat little house on the edge of the plum orchard. On the gravel in front of the door, amongst pots of cheerful pink geraniums, a little girl is stroking Lafite, who has stretched himself out luxuriously to bask in the warmth of the sun. As I walk up the path, Lafite scrambles to his feet and comes to greet me, purring and winding himself around my shins. The little girl watches me for a moment, and I have an impression of big, serious brown eyes set in a pale heart-shaped face which is framed by straight brown hair. She turns and darts into the house, reappearing a few seconds later with Mireille.

"Gina my dear, how are you?" Mireille kisses me on either cheek before enveloping me in a warm hug. She looks at my face searchingly. "Yesterday was a sad day, but today is a little more peaceful I think?" She turns to usher forward the little girl. "May I present my granddaughter, Nathalie." The child turns her serious face upwards for the customary kiss on each side.

"Lafite was very much enjoying being stroked by you," I smile.

"Yes," she says. "He is missing Liz" – she pronounces it Lees – "but I am helping Grand'mère look after him and cheer him up."

"Well thank you, he couldn't be among better friends."

"Shall we come to the house with you?" asks Mireille.

I had planned to go on my own, but suddenly the thought of stepping over the threshold alone into that emptiness overwhelms me. "Yes please, I'd like that."

And the company is just what I need, I realise, as Nathalie and Lafite dance ahead of us scattering any ghosts, and Mireille's calm presence at my side dispels the loneliness I had been feeling.

To my relief, the house is pervaded by an air of peace and I feel surprisingly reassured to be standing in the kitchen once again, the calm tick of the clock on the mantel above the fireplace stolidly marking time as if nothing has changed.

"She was lying here on the floor when I found her," says Mireille softly. "I'd come over for my customary cup of afternoon tea. It was Liz who introduced me to this most civilised of English customs. The kettle was still warm, so she can't have been there long. She sensed it was coming. She'd been getting things organised for the past few months. I helped her take some bags to the dump and others, of clothes and whatever else might be of use, to the church. It was important to her to leave everything in order."

Tears spring to my eyes. "When I was here, she wasn't well. I told her to go to the doctor. I should have stayed, taken her to the hospital maybe..."

Mireille puts a steadying hand on my arm. "Which she would have refused to do." She smiles at me and hands me a tissue from her pocket. "You know how strong-minded your aunt always was – stubborn as a mule. She had made up her mind and wanted to do this on her own terms. She got what she had hoped for, which was a wonderful quality of life right up to the end, and to die in her own home. Not in a hospital, full of tubes, nor to moulder in a nursing home amongst strangers. She was ready to go, you know."

We wander through the rooms, where everything is neatly ordered. The heaps of papers have disappeared from the study and only a few items of clothing hang in the wardrobe in Liz's bedroom.

"She just kept what she might need from day to day," explains Mireille. "Would you like me to clear out these last few things and take them to the church? It's a sad job, getting rid of something as personal as clothes, and so it might be easier for me to do. As long as you and your mother don't want any of it, of course."

I think of Mum's elegantly conservative clothes in neutral colours, a far cry from Liz's more flamboyant taste. "I'd be grateful, if you wouldn't mind doing it," I reply. "I already have a few things that she gave me to remember her by."

We make our way back down to the kitchen. Nathalie and Lafite, bored at the thought of wasting time inside, are in the courtyard, the cat watching with eagle eyes a lizard that has plastered itself to the wall. The little girl is sitting on the step making daisy chains. With a crunch of gravel, Celia's car pulls up and the quiet of the moment is shattered.

We discuss practicalities for a while – Celia and Mireille between them will keep an eye on things until the lawyer has finalised the will and I decide what to do with the house.

"Take your time my dear," says Mireille as she takes her leave. "It meant a lot to Liz to leave you the house, but she didn't want it to be a burden. You must do whatever you feel is right for you."

And I watch as the old lady makes her way down the drive, accompanied by the little girl wearing a crown of daisies, and the big black cat.

*

My mind is still in France when I return to the office on Monday morning. On automatic pilot, I open my emails and realise I'm reading one from Roddy. 'So sorry to hear of your aunt's death - saw her obit. Presume you must be in France. Thinking of you. Love R.'

It's the 'Love R' that really gets my attention. As I'm mulling this over, my phone beeps, signalling an incoming text message and I fish it out of my bag. From: Roddy. 'Call me when u get this. X'.

Heavens, what's going on? Love R? A kiss? My mind starts to race.

I'm still in a state of distraction when Harry leans out of his office and says, "Gina, can I ask you to come through please?"

And so it hardly sinks in at first when he tells me that the company has been bought by one of the big chains. And he's going to have to make me redundant.

Chapter 4.

Of course I call Roddy. Drowning in grief, shock and despondency, who wouldn't reach out to grab the emotional life preserver he is holding out to me?

We meet in the local Italian restaurant, familiar territory since we used to come here on Friday nights to celebrate the end of the working week, relaxing over plates of spaghetti puttanesca and a bottle of house plonk. Roddy is already there when I arrive – notable in itself as he is usually late as a matter of course – and stands up solicitously to embrace me as I reach the table. He orders a bottle of wine, a Barolo from the top end of the wine list rather than our usual Valpolicella and I am pleased and cautiously flattered that he is making such an effort. Where is this going, I wonder, trying to ignore the glow of hope that has rekindled itself in my heart. Have he and Camilla split up? I'd forgotten how very good-looking he is, and how utterly charming he can be when not otherwise distracted. I ask Roddy, with a smile of irony at the normality of the question, how his week has been.

Roddy is Director of Sponsorship for an events company. When you come down to it, this means he sells advertising. But of course it would never do to voice such a vulgar thought. The job mainly involves wining and dining contacts made though the Old Boy networks of the public schools of southern England and persuading them, in the most gentlemanly manner of course, to part with large dollops of money to have their companies' names displayed at polo matches, rugby fixtures and regattas. Apparently at the moment things aren't going too well, due to the fact that the economy has taken a sharp nosedive and it is proving, Roddy admits over his bresaiola and rocket salad, to be a bit of a bore.

"But that's enough about me. More importantly, how are you?" he asks, reaching a sympathetic hand across the table to hold mine. The glow of hope flickers into a small flame. "I was so sorry to hear about your job. Still, in the big scheme of things it's funny how it's worked out really isn't it? You've obviously reached an important crossroads in your life. What are you planning on doing next, now you have carte blanche?"

I'm surprised that he sees my current situation in quite such exciting and positive terms, but Roddy's always been an optimist and perhaps he's right – I should see this as an opportunity for a fresh start rather than having the distinct feeling that I am being swept rapidly up a creek without a paddle.

He gazes across at me over the flickering tealight and the bottles of oil and vinegar as I describe the calls I've made and the copies of my CV I've sent out, completely fruitlessly to date. "The wine industry seems to be taking a similar battering," I explain. "Like your sponsorship, I suppose wine is seen as a luxury item, so when times get tight it's one of the first things people cut back on. The supermarkets will carry on undercutting everyone else so they'll be ok. But I don't expect Wainright's will be the only independent wine merchant to disappear. And at least they were bought out. Some of the independents are sure to go under. Every wine buyer in the country will be sitting tight and trying to hang on to their job. So it looks like I'm going to be a lady of leisure for the foreseeable future." I try to make light of my situation, which actually sounds even more dire when I have to explain it like this.

The waiter appears with our plates of pasta and then suggestively brandishes an over-sized pepper-grinder in my direction. "Pepper for the bella signorina?" he asks, and Roddy and I smile at each other over this well-worn joke. Roddy waves him away and pours me some more of the dark red wine.

"Well I'd like to propose a toast," he says with a flourish of his own glass. "Here's to ladies of leisure. I was sorry to hear about your Aunt Liz, of course, but talk about good timing. Presumably she's left everything to you? Bit of a silver lining as it turns out, eh?"

For a few seconds I continue to smile as I try to work out what he can possibly mean. And then as realisation dawns, a wave of icy cold water washes over the blaze of hope that, I have to admit, was now burning brightly within me, extinguishing it completely. "I'm sorry?" I say coldly. "I'm not sure I quite follow."

Roddy continues breezily, "Well, she must have been pretty minted, and you were certainly her nearest and dearest relation, just like a daughter in fact, so surely she's come up trumps just when you need it most. I always did like the old girl – a great character."

His mobile phone, on the pink table cloth beside a half-eaten bread stick, suddenly vibrates. He glances down at it and then smoothly – too smoothly – returns his gaze to my face. "Gina?" he asks, as I glare at him in cold fury.

I reach over and pick up his phone. On the illuminated square of the screen is a little yellow envelope and next to it the name Camilla.

"Ah yes," I say, "how is the lovely Camilla these days? Still your landlady? Or did you finally strap on a pair of balls and decide to stand on your own two feet for a change? No?" I continue, as his gaze flickers uncertainly to the plate of food in front of him. "So you're still living with her, but thought it would be worth checking me out again in case I'd suddenly become a better financial proposition? I should have known. The trouble with you, Roderick Hamilton, is that you are, and always will be, a complete arsehole. Thanks for supper, but sorry, I've just remembered I'd rather be at home cleaning the loo than wasting one more second of my life in your company."

Shaking with rage, I push back my chair and stalk out of the restaurant, Italian waiters with their over-sized pepper grinders scattering before me as I go. Not such a bella signorina after all, evidently.

My fury propels me to my front door and up the stairs to my flat before I collapse sobbing on the sofa and lie there, breakers of humiliation, pain and grief crashing over me as I contemplate the twisted pile of wreckage that is my life.

*

Sleep has now become as elusive as a reliable man or a steady job.

I contemplate each night with dread as it stretches before me, a dark desert to be crossed alone. And I know that in the shadows lurk my worried thoughts, waiting to ambush me and harry me, nipping at my heels like a pack of wild dogs. Some evenings I drift asleep in front of the television before dragging myself groggily into bed an hour or so later, only to lie there wider awake than ever the minute my head hits the pillow. Sometimes, relieved that another night is over, I fall into a deep sleep just as dawn is breaking, only to flounder in a quicksand of troubled dreams, which relinquish their grip on my mind only reluctantly when I wake, leaving me queasy and emotionally drained.

One of these dreams stays with me with particular clarity. I'm trying to get to France – I have to get to France to see Liz urgently – but am held up at every turn. Firstly I have work to finish (ha!), then I jump into a taxi to get to the airport only to find Roddy sitting in it. He insists we go back to his place to pick up his suitcase. I realise we've missed the plane, so I go to catch a bus to the station, but there's one just pulling away and I run to catch it but my legs are like lead weights and my lungs constrict so that I can hardly move. I push on though and get to the station. The Eurostar is – miraculously – still there and I go to buy a ticket. But there's a long queue and it's not moving. I crane my head to see who's holding it up and Roddy turns to smile at me from the front of the line. Weak-kneed with relief, I go up to him, but he turns away. Then I see he has bought two tickets and I know the second one is not for me. In desperation, I get on the train anyway just as it pulls away from the platform. But instead of whizzing soundlessly through the countryside, it seems to have developed the same problem as my legs and drags itself along laboriously. I get out and miraculously find myself at Sainte Foy – hooray, nearly there, hang on Liz, I'm coming. I force my leaden limbs to carry me up the hill and finally I turn into the drive under the oaks. But the courtyard is empty and the trees are skeletons and I know I'm too late. All I can hear is my desperate, gasping breath and then a magpie flutters down from one of the trees and starts towards me with menacing intent. It gives a rasping cry and I wake with a start.

And I really am gasping for breath, and there really is a magpie calling in the trees in one of the neighbouring gardens.

I lie there for a while, trying to calm my breathing and gather my thoughts. Thank goodness I don't have to go to work in this state, I think, I'd never be able to function properly. And then I consider this thought a little more rationally and realise that I've lost sight of the wood for the trees. Or maybe I'm putting the chicken before the egg. Whichever, I need to get a grip.

I get up and go through to the kitchen. Opening the fridge door, I gaze at an unappetising heel of stale bread and a single pot of yoghurt which, on closer inspection, turns out to be about a week past its sell-by date.

The phone lies on the counter beside me and, almost without thinking, I pick it up and dial. "Hi Mum," I say, "how are you?"

"Oh hello darling, just getting ready to go out actually. What are you doing today?"

"Nothing much. Just wondering if I could pop over sometime?"

"Well I'm going shopping this morning and then I've got Bridge this afternoon," she replies breezily.

"OK, well another day then," I try hard to keep the tremor in my voice from spilling over into something unstoppable.

There's a pause.

"Are you alright darling?"

I swallow hard and suddenly find that I can't get the words out because if I open my mouth I'll start to cry and I don't think I'll ever be able to stop.

"Actually the shopping can wait," says my mother briskly. "Come straight over. Or shall I come to you instead?"

I take a deep breath. "I'll come to you. Be nice to have a change of scene," I say into the phone with a watery smile.

"Alright darling, see you in half an hour. I'll get the coffee on."

*

"It's such a lovely day, let's take this into the garden," says Mum, putting two mugs of coffee onto a tray beside a Royal Doulton plate bearing a semicircle of Digestive biscuits. The familiarity is comforting. Instead of sitting on the terrace beside the wall of the house, she leads the way across the lawn to Dad's bench. We sit and she offers me the plate of biscuits. I shake my head and she says kindly, "Come on Gina, you look as if you haven't eaten properly in days. Or slept either, come to that. Take one and tell me what's on your mind." Balancing her mug of coffee on the arm of the bench, she reaches over and takes my hand.

And we sit there for a while as the tears pour silently down my face and she waits patiently and calmly until the torrent turns to a trickle. Then, releasing my hand, she pulls a neatly folded handkerchief from her sleeve and passes it to me. "My poor darling girl," she says, which sets me off again, but I'm almost cried out now, so after a minute or two I blow my nose and find that the heavy, oppressive weight of my grief has been washed away in the flood and now I am left empty and exhausted, but calmer.

"I'm going to have to sell Liz's house," I blurt out, gazing sightlessly at the blue of the southerly skies before us. "If I sell it, I can pay off the mortgage on the flat, so at least I won't lose that as well. Then hopefully my redundancy money will tide me over, if I'm careful, until I can find another job."

My mother looks at me appraisingly. "I see. Is that really what you want to do? It doesn't sound much fun to me."

I sniff and then blow my nose again on the crumpled handkerchief which I've been clutching in my fist. "Well, I don't exactly have any choices at the moment," I say bitterly.

"Nonsense darling. Choices are exactly what you have. This is a wonderful opportunity for you." I start to interrupt, but she holds up a hand. "Now hear me out. I know you've been through a horrible time, and I'm not surprised you're knocked sideways. You feel as if you've lost everything just at the moment."

A sob escapes me and she takes my hand again.

"But in reality you've gained enormous freedom and that's not something that happens to everyone in life. This is a wonderful chance for you to take yourself off and do something completely different."

"But I can't sell the flat here," I say. "The way things are right now nobody's buying." I feel a flash of irritation towards my mother. It's OK for her, sitting here in her comfortable cocoon protected from the economic gales that are howling just beyond her front gate. She honestly hasn't a clue about managing money and the reality of other people's financial problems.

"Well darling," she replies brightly, "I don't think it's the time to sell the house in France either. If des-res properties in commuter belt Arundel aren't selling then tumbledown farmhouses in the depths of rural France are unlikely to be going like hot cakes either. And with the Euro so strong against Sterling at the moment you won't have queues of Brits lining up to buy over there."

I turn to look at my mother in astonishment. Blimey, not quite so clueless after all, it seems.

"Let's face it," she continues. "This isn't just a little economic blip, it's likely to be a serious recession for at least a year. And despite the resulting increase in the number of people drowning their sorrows, the wine trade is going to be going through rocky times for the foreseeable future, so if the thought of sitting in your flat scraping by on benefits appeals then by all means go ahead. I just think you can find a more positive solution to all this, a bright girl like you.

"You're right that no-one's buying at the moment, so why not rent out your flat. That way your mortgage will be covered. And apparently the rental market is booming, especially in places like Arundel. Go and spend some time in France. You have somewhere to stay that you love. Your redundancy money will tide you over for a while and I'll help out too if need be. You've always wanted to get your Master of Wine qualification and you can easily do it from there and come back to sit the exams when you're ready. Indeed, what better place to be to immerse yourself in wine. Within reason of course," she finishes with a smile.

We sit in silence for a few seconds while I take all this in. I turn to her with a wry smile. "Heavens, you have been giving my life a good deal of thought."

"Of course I have darling, I'm your mother." She looks off into the distance. "Dad would have given you the same advice you know. He'd have been delighted if you got your MW. Now," she says, gathering up the mugs and tray, "I'm going to leave you to sit in the sun and think things over while I get our lunch ready."

*

As I take my leave I hug my mother warmly. "Thanks Mum," I say and she smiles and strokes the side of my face with a gesture that is utterly tender.

"You're a gorgeous girl Gina, and a wonderful daughter. I'm so proud of you, you know. Now get out there and start living." Then she bends her head to rummage in her red Mulberry bag for her car keys.

And so we each get into our cars, my mother to go off to her afternoon of Bridge, sandwiches and small talk and I to see a letting agent and get a life.

Chapter 5.

I catch the overnight ferry to St Malo and then drive the whole way in one day, retracing the homeward journey I made in the early spring. And now, strangely, this is my homeward journey. My flat is let on a year's lease to a young couple, unable to get financing to buy their own home now that the banks have stopped lending. A year ago they'd have been handed a hundred percent mortgage with no problem at all. A year ago I was still in my nice safe job. A year ago Roddy was living in my flat. A year ago Liz was here in her house.

The car pulls into the courtyard and I turn off the engine, sitting for a few seconds to let the realisation that I'm here sink in and to allow the engine noise, which is still ringing in my ears, to subside.

It's early June, but feels like high summer already, and the leaves on the lime trees are a dense, dark green. As my hearing adjusts, I realise the sound I am hearing is coming from their fresh-scented pale yellow flowers which are abuzz with bees in the golden warmth of the evening. The geraniums in their pots are dry and dusty. I ease my stiff limbs out of the driver's seat and dig in my handbag for the keys. Dragging my heavy suitcase and holdall from the boot, I unlock the kitchen door and push it open, stepping into the cool half-light. I open shutters and windows to allow the evening air to flood the house, the soundtrack of cicadas and birdsong exorcising the silence and emptiness that haunt the rooms.

I make my way upstairs to Liz's bedroom and hesitate before opening the door. The bed has been stripped and the duvet is folded neatly back over the end of the bedstead. I cross to the wardrobe and turn the key. It's empty. Mireille has been true to her word and disposed of the rest of Liz's clothes. I pull on the cords that open the roof lights and let the fresh air in and a couple of angrily buzzing flies out. I haven't decided where I'm going to sleep, but now I'm in here it seems more comforting, closer to Liz somehow, to make this my room.

I'm making my way back downstairs to fetch some sheets from the armoire that stands in the hall, when I hear the crunch of footsteps in the gravel of the courtyard. Going into the kitchen, I find Lafite sitting looking at me expectantly. There's a gentle tap at the doorway and I turn to see Mireille standing on the threshold, a wicker basket on one arm and a plastic carrier bag in the other hand. Bending to put these down, she comes to embrace me warmly.

"*Ma chère* Gina, how good to see you've arrived safely," she beams, her eyes crinkling in her wrinkled brown face. I look at her, a little surprised. I hadn't told anyone down here that I was coming. "Aha," she laughs, "surely you didn't think your arrival would go unannounced and unnoticed? You are living in the country now, my dear, so you'll have to get used to everyone knowing your business even before you know it yourself! I heard from Madame Everett, who heard from your mother, that you would be arriving today. Lafite and I have been watching out for your car. No doubt Madame Everett will be round to call on you tomorrow, but I wanted to be the first to welcome you this evening."

She picks up the basket and bag and sets them on the kitchen table. "Here are a few things to keep you going tonight and for your breakfast tomorrow, until you have a chance to get to the shops." She takes a long loaf of crusty bread, some butter and eggs from the basket. "And here are the very last of the cherries from my tree. The season's just over. There's a jar of my cherry jam too. And of course a bottle of wine to celebrate your homecoming. I'm so pleased you've decided to come and live here. Liz would have been delighted."

Hmm, the international grapevine certainly seems to have been busy. So much for independence. But secretly I feel pleased at the invisible web of support these redoubtable ladies have been weaving behind my back.

"Here are Lafite's things, feeding dish, water bowl, some food. He's been happy with me, but I know he'll be even more pleased to be back where he belongs. He often pops back here to visit you know – I think he's been waiting for you."

"Mireille, you are so kind, thank you. Will you stay and have a glass of wine?"

"Not today my dear. I know you'll be tired after your long journey and want to get settled in. I'll leave you for now, but come and visit me whenever you wish. You know where I am if you need anything."

With another hug, she picks up the empty basket and ambles off up the drive. Lafite winds himself about my ankles and then gazes up at my face, giving a plaintive-sounding meow. "Supper time is it? Come on then," I say. "And I think I'd better give those poor geraniums some water before they die of thirst."

It's good to have some purposeful activities that need doing. I had dreaded the silence and emptiness of my first evening here but now I bustle around, watering the pots in the courtyard, wiping dust off the kitchen surfaces, and making up the bed in Liz's room with crisply ironed sheets from the armoire that smell of fresh air, sunshine and lavender.

The sun has set by the time I sit at the table on the terrace with a glass of wine and a plate of scrambled eggs before me. The wine Mireille brought me is a bottle of Clairet, the local rosé, and I hold up the glass to admire its colour. I remember helping Dad re-fill the bird feeder in our garden in the autumn, and hear him saying, "Look at those bullfinches Gina. A good rosé should be the same

70

colour as their stomachs, precisely that gentle coral pink." This wine is a bolder colour, more the orange-red of a robin's breast, and its chilled, dry complexity is thoroughly refreshing.

Lafite sits on the wall cleaning his whiskers and I feel a deep calm descend as I watch the sky turn from gold to black. The last swallows flit by, catching a few final flies in the warm evening air before slipping into their nests under the eaves for the night. In the oak trees an owl hoots. I raise my glass. "Thank you Liz," I whisper.

*

Next morning I'm sitting at the desk in Liz's study – my study, I mean. The reality of my new situation is only slowly sinking in.

I've been speaking to the phone company and feel a huge sense of achievement, not to mention relief, as I've managed to negotiate the tortuous push-button system, (frequently pressing the button to "*répéter les options*" as I strain to understand the alternatives being offered me in rapid-fire French), and am assured by the real human being I finally managed to speak to that my internet connection will be up and running in a week's time. I feel somewhat stranded without this link to the wide world and I'm going to need it for starting to plan the studying I need to do as I embark on the Masters of Wine programme. Not to mention keeping up with the latest electronic gossip from Annie and my other friends across the Channel.

I jump slightly at the sound of tyres on the gravel outside. Looking at my watch, I smile. 10.30. This must be Celia coming to check up on me. She hasn't wasted much time. I thought she'd consider afternoon tea a more socially acceptable point at which to call. But then looking out of the window I see a huge cream-coloured Mercedes cruise into the courtyard like an ocean liner, dwarfing my little car as it docks in the shade of the lime trees.

As I watch, a dapper, middle-aged man steps out, wearing a pair of trousers that would be described in the ads at the back of the Daily Telegraph as 'permapress slacks', and a navy blazer with two rows of glittering gold buttons down the front. He pauses to look up appraisingly at the facade of the house and then smoothes back his suspiciously shiny hair at either temple. He walks briskly to the front door and knocks on it with three confidently sharp raps.

Flustered, I hesitate, ruefully aware of the fact that this morning I pulled on the first clothes that came to hand from the top of my holdall. I'm dressed, skimpily, for unpacking, cleaning, weeding and, hopefully, a little sitting in the sun in between it all, in a halter-neck top and a pair of worn jeans that I now deeply regret cutting off at upper-thigh level last summer. It's a look that's definitely more Daisy Duke than Doris Day.

Can I pretend I'm not here? But to my horror the man is now opening the door and he sticks his head through to call. "'Allo. Ees zere anybodee zere?"

I draw myself up to my full five foot six, tall enough to look most Frenchmen in the eye, and march out of the study to confront him.

"*Bonjour monsieur*," I say, hoping the iciness of my tone will freeze his over-confidence. But not a bit of it. With a broad smile, which displays two rows of slightly yellowing teeth, he steps across the threshold to shake my hand. I try not to blush as he gives my outfit an appraising glance, but feel my cheeks flush with embarrassment as he grins appreciatively.

"Mademoiselle. Please excuse this intrusion," he says in heavily-accented English. "I am Laurent Dubois. I 'ave come to welcome you to the region and to extend my sympathies to you for the sad loss of your aunt." His cheerful smile and jaunty tone suggest that this sadness is somewhat less than heartfelt in his case.

"*Merci, Monsieur Dubois, c'est très gentil*," I reply, continuing firmly in French. "Do you live nearby?" His name is ringing a faint bell, but I can't quite place him.

"In Sainte Foy," comes the reply, again in English. "I 'ave known your aunt for many years."

Suddenly the penny drops. "*Ah oui*, Dubois Immobilier in the rue Victor Hugo."

Of course. In the plate glass window, amongst the details of properties for sale, there's a large photo displaying the same slicked-back hair and toothy smile and beneath this the words 'English spoken'.

With a flourish, he pulls a business card from the breast pocket of his blazer. "At your service, mademoiselle. If you are wishing to sell this property, I 'ave a client who might be interested in buying it. Of course, you would need to do some work on it first. The paintwork needs re-doing and you may wish to consider replacing the windows with plastic frames which are so much more desirable. The roof needs some work on it as well. I can give you the telephone number of my brother-in-law 'oo is in the building trade, if you wish."

I'm a little startled at the directness of his approach, to say the least, and feel my face flushing again, this time with annoyance rather than embarrassment. "That's very kind of you, but I'm not selling at the moment."

"I also 'andle rentals. Although you will still 'ave to do the repairs to get the 'ouse into a better condition. There are not many English renting long-term at the moment. And without a swimming pool it will be 'ard to get 'oliday rentals."

"*Merci*," I reply, firmly persisting with my French. It's starting to feel like a competition to see who will submit first linguistically, and I'm damned if I'm going to be the one to give in. "But I'm not renting either. I'm going to live here."

Laurent Dubois looks me up and down approvingly once again and this time his gaze is, frankly, lascivious. "Bravo mademoiselle, that is good news for our little corner of the world. And you will still need the services of my brother-in-law no doubt. But per'aps I can be of assistance in 'andling the necessary works for you." As if to demonstrate his 'andling skills here and now, he pauses to place a slightly damp hand on my bare arm, just a little too near the cotton of my halter-neck top which suddenly feels dangerously flimsy.

I look down at his hand with what I hope is eloquent disdain, but he doesn't remove it. OK, no more Mrs Nice Guy. I take his sticky paw between thumb and forefinger and firmly remove it, raising my eyebrows and looking pointedly at his gold wedding ring. "*Vraiment*, Monsieur Dubois, I assure you I have no need of the services of either you or your brother-in-law, nor anyone else just at present. My aunt lived in this house for over thirty years and if it was OK for her, it's OK for me. Now thank you for your visit, but if you'll excuse me I have work to do. My regards to Madame Dubois. *Au revoir*."

The estate agent, apparently unabashed, grins at me. But his final retort is in French, so I congratulate myself on winning that battle at least. "Ah, *les Anglaises*. Always with a closed mind. You don't understand how pleasant our little French ways can be. And I assure you," he finishes with an upward glance, "you'll regret not seeing to that roof. Welcome to the region, mademoiselle"

And with a jaunty mock salute he climbs back into his cruise ship of a car and sails off, with unhurried insouciance, down the drive.

*

I regale Celia Everett with the story of Monsieur Dubois' visit when she comes to call that afternoon, arriving with diplomatic punctiliousness at 3.40 precisely. She laughs at my indignation. "Gina my dear, Laurent Dubois is notorious throughout the area for his extra-marital dalliances. He tries it on with every English woman he meets, so it's no surprise that he couldn't resist the charms of one so young and evidently unattached."

"And indeed underdressed," I add with a rueful laugh.

"He's originally from Paris, which the locals would say explains a lot. He married a girl from Sainte Foy and has some kind of dubious business partnership going with her brother, who's in the building trade. I feel sorry for Madame Dubois. His 'little French ways' are common knowledge throughout the neighbourhood. I wouldn't say he's at all typical though, so don't worry, you're not going to be besieged at every turn by amorous, adulterous Frenchmen."

"Well it's disgusting," I retort, thinking of my own recent humiliation at the hands of that two-timing ratfink Roddy. "Think of the hurt it must cause his wife."

"Darling, I know. But don't worry, we'll find you a nice, steady unattached man. Speaking of which, I bumped into Nigel Yates at the post office this morning. He was very pleased indeed to hear you've come back here to live," she says archly.

I sigh and roll my eyes in exasperation. "Celia, it's really very kind of you, but I don't think Nigel's exactly my type. In fact right now I've had enough of men and their 'little ways', both English and French. I just need a bit of space. And anyway, I'm going to be too busy now with my MW coursework to have time for anything more."

"OK, OK," she holds up her hands in mock defence, her fingers securely claimed by the heavy diamonds of her engagement and eternity rings which sparkle in the afternoon sunshine. "I'll back off the matchmaking. You've certainly come to the right place if space is what you're looking for. Don't be lonely now, will you? You know Hugh and I are just along the road whenever you feel like some company."

She stands to take her leave and I give her a fond hug.

"I know Celia, thanks. You're so kind and it really is very reassuring to know you're there. Once I've got things sorted out a little more I'll give you a call. Perhaps you and Hugh can come to supper one evening."

"We'd love to, but no rush. Take your time to get yourself settled in. It's a big adjustment for you. We hope you'll be very happy here."

I bend down to stroke Lafite, who's curled up on a chair beside us. "I am, and I've got Lafite for company – he's much more reliable than any human male."

*

That night I lie awake as usual, mulling over the conversations I've had with today's visitors. The moon isn't helping my sleepless state either. It must be almost full. I've left the blinds open and its white light streams in through the windows in the roof, illuminating the room as clearly as one of Liz's black and white prints. With a flicker of annoyance as I recall the estate agent's damp hand on my bare skin, I turn restlessly onto my side, trying to find a more relaxing position in which sleep may be possible.

Reaching for my watch on the bedside table, my gaze falls on the photo in the heavy silver frame. Six magpies in a tree, their black tails outlined clearly against a white sky.

And then, my detached mind registering the fact almost dreamily, I realise there is one more. Sitting within the cross-hatch of the branches, its straight tail feathers look like just another twig. But there, above the tail, is the unmistakable rounded bulk of the bird's body and head.

Suddenly I'm sitting bolt upright in the bed. Seven. A secret never to be told. Even as I turn the frame over and ease back the clips that have rusted slightly into the velvet backing, I'm telling myself not to be silly. There won't be anything here. It's just a photo of a few birds, not some melodramatic message from beyond the grave.

In the moonlight I prise a sheet of thick photographic paper from the frame.

And I'm looking into my father's eyes.

They are smiling with a loving, tender gaze, right into the camera, as he leans forward, lips parted, to say something to the person taking the picture. Across one corner of the print, in his handwriting which is as familiar to me as my own, is a message. It reads, 'For Liz – my love, always, David.'

As if the look in his dark, moonlit eyes hadn't already said it all.

Chapter 6.

I once read an article in a magazine about a prison in South Africa where the gangs-and-drugs culture was so tough the terrified and powerless guards would lock themselves into their offices at night, allowing the prisoners to take over until daybreak. It strikes me now that this is a bit like the mind of an insomniac. After dark, the lunatics take over the asylum and irrational anxiety and hopeless fear rule.

Because there is a kind of madness that comes with insomnia. The connections in the brain, which in the light of day allow it to function quite rationally, somehow become scrambled. The normally unthinkable becomes perfectly possible, if not probable. The doubts and fears, banished in daylight to dark corners, come creeping out and push any sensible thoughts away into some unreachable chasm.

Tonight there's plenty of food for thought, and any chance of sleep makes its escape out of the skylights above my head, the way lit by stark white moonbeams.

At first I try to come up with a sensible, rational explanation for the photo. Perhaps it's just someone who looks like him. (But it's his writing and he's signed his name). Perhaps it was a photo meant for my mother. (But it's inscribed to Liz). Perhaps it's just a token of friendship. ('My love, always?' The look in his eyes?) Perhaps it's a forgotten memento from an affair before he met my mother. (Still in a silver frame beside Liz's bed?)

I rack my brains for snippets of family history which might help me date the picture. Liz wasn't at my parents' wedding, that I know from photos in a heavy old cream leather album, embossed at the corners with overlapping gold lines, that I used to love to pore over when I was little. I once asked Mum why Liz wasn't amongst the small crowd of guests posing on the registry office steps and she said her sister had been working in New York at the time and that transatlantic travel wasn't nearly as easy, nor as cheap, as it is nowadays. According to Mum, Dad had swept her off her feet and asked her to marry him just a couple of months after they'd met at a dance in London. "She was the most beautiful girl in the room," had chimed in my father with a fond smile. "I can still remember the dress she was wearing and she had her hair pinned up in a most becoming style."

I don't think my father met his sister-in-law until after he and Mum were married.

I pick up the photo and look at it again, bracing myself for the pang of pain and betrayal I know I'll feel. I turn on the bedside lamp to look at the image more clearly, the familiar, well-loved features seeming like those of a stranger in this bewildering new context.

His face is young and fresh, the photo taken years before lines etched themselves across his forehead and grey hairs eroded the dark sand of the hair at his temples. This same face gazes out from pages and pages of pictures in the cream leather album. Engagement photos. Wedding photos. Photos of him cradling his newborn baby daughter in his arms. Him and Mum. Him and me.

I put the picture back, face down, on the bedside table and reach over to turn off the light. On second thoughts, I think I'll leave it on, so that the dark shadows that threaten to crowd in on me as the moon continues on its way across the starlit sky, will be kept pinned back against the walls where they belong. I turn over, trying to find a cooler patch of pillow to cushion my burning cheek and my overheated brain.

And then I think, 'What if Liz is really my mother, but in some strange twist of events she gave me to her younger sister?' I hear an echo of Roddy's voice saying "You were just like a daughter to the old girl."

But in my mind's eye I can see, as clearly as if it were beside me on the bedside table too, another photo from the same old album. Mum lying back in a hospital bed, propped up against crisp white pillows, with a small bundle tightly wrapped in a pink honeycombed blanket, held carefully in her arms.

Her hair, usually immaculately set, is dishevelled and on her exhausted face are written pain and love in equal quantities. "It was such a difficult labour," she'd said. "In the end they had to do an emergency caesarean. So it was no more bikinis for me from then on."

As the long night wears on and the pool of yellow light from the bedside lamp starts to dissolve into the paleness of dawn, the whirl of thoughts slows and then comes to a silent stop.

And then, all other possibilities exhausted, I'm left with the certain knowledge that my father and my aunt, two of the people I have trusted and loved most dearly in my life, have betrayed my mother and me with a secret love of their own.

*

Now I'm angry. I'm angry at Dad and at Liz for obvious reasons. I'm angry too because they've both gone and left me alone with the fact of their affair but no way of getting the further explanation that they owe me. I'm angry at my mother, and I'm not quite sure why. And I'm absolutely furious with myself for being so naive as to believe that anyone on this godforsaken planet could ever be faithful.

My anger – and the sudden horrific thought that maybe my father and my aunt used to lie together in this very bed, yikes, don't even start to go there - gives me energy and I briskly get up and dressed. Then I clatter downstairs, Lafite giving me a look of baleful reproach as he flees before me, to Liz's study.

I pull open drawer after drawer in her desk and filing cabinets, searching for letters, diaries, anything that will expose what really happened between her and Dad. But she's done a thorough job of clearing everything out – I think again, coldly this time, of those black bin bags – and there's nothing much left. I race back up the stairs, taking them two at a time, to the bedroom and wrench open chests and cupboards. Again nothing, except for the neatly folded sheets of brown paper that line the shelves and drawers. I lift these up but beneath them is dusty wood, scattered with a few dried grains of faintly-scented lavender.

I turn to the photos lying on the bedside table. Picking them up, I go back downstairs, moving more slowly this time, and into the kitchen. Lafite is sitting patiently by his dish and looks up calmly as I enter. I put the photos carefully on the kitchen table and come over, chastened, to stroke his broad old head. "Sorry, did I scare you earlier? None of this is your fault, you poor old boy. I wish you could tell me what you know though." He slowly blinks his eyes in forgiveness, given that it looks as though breakfast is imminent, and I pour food into his chipped bowl.

As I drink my coffee and spread cherry jam on a hunk of slightly stale bread, I look at the two photos on the table beside my plate. It strikes me that there are three alternatives here.

The first is that Liz meant to 'clear away' the photo before she died, as she had methodically tidied away the rest of her life, but had hung on to it and then been taken sooner than she'd expected. It's a distinct possibility.

The second is that she never meant the photo to be discovered beneath the picture of the magpies, which seems unlikely and risky.

And the third, which dawns on me as clearly as the bright sunshine which is now streaming in through the window as I chew a mouthful of crust, almost unconsciously savouring the sweet tartness of the black cherries, is that she meant me to find it. That in fact it is a message to me from beyond the grave. But why not just put it in an envelope addressed with my name?

Because it's still a secret never to be told. But perhaps Liz wanted me to know, now that both she and Dad are gone.

And maybe the person she wants to protect is not her niece, but her sister.

Chapter 7.

When the going gets tough, the tough get cleaning. I suppose it's a way of trying to impose some sense of control when every other area of my life has collapsed into uncertainty and disarray. I'm still awaiting the arrival of the France Telecom engineer to sort out my internet connection and I need to do something to distract myself from the thoughts, threatening to verge on the unhealthily obsessive now, that go round and round in my head. Like a hamster running desperately on a wheel in its cage, I'm getting nowhere fast.

Cleaning is a good way of using up the angry energy that's fizzing in my veins, refusing to allow me to settle down peacefully with a good book. And, if I'm honest, there's always the possibility that I might uncover some more bits of the jigsaw and begin to piece together exactly what went on between Liz and Dad. So I set to work methodically, room by room, scrubbing, dusting, polishing. I even open up and clean the sitting room (scarcely used) and dining room (never used), moving the ancient, solid pieces of furniture to hoover beneath them and sending long-undisturbed spiders scuttling frantically for new cover. Other than dust and cobwebs, I find nothing.

When I've finished cleaning, I start washing. Perhaps I'm trying to wipe the slate clean so that I can live in a state of happy denial and transform my family history back into the neat storybook facsimile it used to be. I wash bedding and cushions and chair covers, hanging them to dry on the line stretched between two apple trees in the garden. The turnaround is gratifyingly fast in the hot sun so I work unremittingly, dragging load after load out of the machine, carrying armfuls of dry, sun-warmed fabric from the line back into the kitchen and sweating over the ironing board where clouds of hissing, angry steam from the iron create the perfect backing track to my mood.

After several days of this, I smooth the freshly laundered *toile de jouy* bedspread over the mattress in the spare room and stand back to survey my handiwork. There's nothing else to wash or dust or polish. I regret the fact that there are no curtains at the windows, other than the small ones under the eaves in the bedroom upstairs which I laundered yesterday, that would have kept me going for a few more days. I move to the window to close the shutters against the midday heat that's now building to a stifling crescendo of sun-glare and cricket song, the humidity making my t-shirt cling limply to my clammy skin.

Triumphantly, I realise that here's my next project. The shutters are in dire need of a fresh coat of paint. They are a sun-cracked red which has faded with a drab brown tinge, like a bottle of old wine that's gone past the point of drinkability. While I'm at it, I think I'll change the colour completely. Make my mark on the house. And, yes I know, symbolically try to blot out a bit more of the past. It's called catharsis, isn't it?

At two o'clock I'm in the car park of the local Mr Bricolage, waiting for the doors to open after the customary two-hour closure for lunch. I choose a sage-green gloss and a selection of brushes, congratulating myself on remembering to add a large bottle of white spirit to my basket. I've never attempted any DIY before, but after all it's not exactly rocket science.

Back at the house, I haul a stepladder out of the shed and drag it across the courtyard to the first set of shutters. It's a good thing only the ground floor windows have them, so I don't have to climb too high. This should be a doddle.

I dip a large brush into the can of pale green paint and begin spreading it over the rusty red. How very satisfying. My soft sage colour spreads easily over the cracked, blistered surface erasing the old and the worn with a beautiful shiny covering. Of course, it's still a bit uneven, but that's good – it looks more weathered and rustic. I wouldn't have wanted to make the shutters look too new. Quite a lot of paint is dripping onto the ground below, so I spread a couple of bin bags out below the ladder. And somehow quite a lot of paint is also getting itself onto the handle of the brush and running down the sides of the tin. And then dripping onto the steps of the ladder and, inexplicably, transferring itself from there to my arms, legs and hair. Good job I remembered the white spirit or I'd look like a soldier in full camouflage gear.

It's a fiddly job trying to paint the ironwork catches and the hinges, and quite a lot of paint also manages to get itself onto the stonework. I go to fetch the white spirit and some kitchen paper and discover I've left a trail of sage green footprints across the recently-scrubbed kitchen floor. It's not easy to get gloss paint off stonework either, I find, and the white spirit just seems to smear it into a bigger stain. I'm starting to get a bit fed up with this job. But I've only painted one pair of shutters and there are... I tally them up in my head... another six sets to do, so twelve more. Oh, plus the big sets on the kitchen door. And the terrace door. And the main door. So that's an additional six which are twice the size. Oh god, I wish I'd never started this. And I'm going to need more paint tomorrow too.

But as I put the ladder away and stick my brushes, thankfully, into an old ice-cream tub filled with white spirit, I pause to look at my day's handiwork. From across the courtyard the spare room shutters don't look bad at all. In fact they look really elegant. And you can hardly see the blobs of paint on the walls around them.

*

That night I collapse into bed after a lukewarm bath to try to take the edge off the now oppressive heat. I've used a nail brush and half a bottle of orange blossom body wash to try to remove the paint and the smell of white spirit from my skin.

I must have successfully worn myself out because I fall into a deep, muggy sleep straight away, drugged by the humid night air which is heavy as a thick woollen blanket.

I'm woken a few hours later by the needling whine of a mosquito. I pull the sheet, the only covering on the bed tonight, over my head. But it's suffocatingly hot like that so after a few minutes I emerge again. I've left the skylights open to try to get a bit of air into the room and then at last, thankfully, I feel the gentle caress of a cool night breeze. I sigh with relief. Now hopefully the mosquito will leave too and there's a chance I'll be able to get back to sleep. I let myself drift off, noting with pleasure the slight ache in my arms and down the back of my calves from today's physical activities. Just relax and sleep will come...

Suddenly there's the most almighty flash of light, blinding even through closed eyelids, and simultaneously a sharp, ear-splitting crack as though some giant axe has split the house in two. My heart leaps against the wall of my ribcage and for a second I think I'm having a cardiac arrest, but the fact that it's now pounding like the pistons on a steam train tells me that it's still working. Indeed it's pumping a massive surge of adrenalin through my veins, definitely inspiring flight rather than fight. I wrench the sheet over my head again, as if a thin piece of cotton is going to protect me from the cacophony that's erupted in the sky above as the violent thunderstorm, which I now realise has been brewing for the last few over-heated days, suddenly explodes directly overhead.

A rush of wind whips the sheet out of my shaking grip and icy drops of hard rain pelt my skin. I leap up, lit like some A-list celebrity by paparazzi flashbulbs of lightning and, gasping with panic and the chill of the raindrops, I grab the pole to yank shut the skylights, hoping desperately that it won't act as a lightning conductor and leave me lying in a frizzled heap on the floor.

The wind swirls, the rain is a deafening roar and the thunder and lightning rage. I grab a top and a pair of jeans off a chair and make my way downstairs, feeling I'll be a little safer there than upstairs with only the roof between me and the storm. My way is lit by the dramatic white flashes of light. When I get to the kitchen door I flick on the light switch and spot Lafite cowering under the table, his fur spiky from the rain. I get down on hands and knees and crawl in to join him I'm only trying to comfort him, honest, I'm not really hiding from a thunderstorm underneath a kitchen table at the age of nearly forty for heaven's sake. And then there's another almighty crash which makes the whole house shake and the lights go out. It's completely black, partly because I'm still under the tent of the (freshly washed-and-ironed) tablecloth and partly because the storm seems to have discharged its entire supply of thunder and lightning with that last blow. So I sit on the floor under the table in the pitch darkness, stroking Lafite and listening to the pouring rain drumming on the roof above us.

*

The next morning the sky is a fresh blue as clear and innocent as the wide eyes of a young child. 'Storm, what storm?' it seems to say. The air is refreshingly cool and I go outside into the courtyard to review the damage. To my relief everything looks OK. And then I spot my lovely green shutters. They appear to have developed some sort of skin problem. Patches of paint are now lifting off like scales, exposing bare wood underneath. Closer inspection shows that last night's rain has made the most of this opportunity and thoroughly soaked the old panels. I prod a brown patch tentatively with a fingernail and it's as soft as damp cardboard. And in the places where the sun is drying out the soaking wood, the paint is splitting and peeling almost before my eyes. Oh god, what a disaster.

But it's nothing like the disaster that is waiting for me round the other side of the house, where one of the tall stone chimney stacks has fallen, taking a large section of moss-covered roof tiles with it as it crashed to the terrace below.

There's a gaping hole in the roof and I dash back inside and upstairs to the bedroom. Through jagged wooden teeth, the ceiling gapes open to the sky. Bits of broken plaster are scattered across the damp bed, washed up in a tide of fine dust. And in the middle of the floor sits the heavy concrete cowl from the top of the chimney.

I run down to the study and pick up the phone, hands shaking as I page through my address book to find Hugh and Celia's number. But the line is dead and I realise that the power is still off and without it the phone won't work. I clatter back upstairs and retrieve my handbag from the debris to try my mobile phone. Damn, I haven't charged it up for days and now the battery's dead. Bloody technology. Well I'll just have to get in the car and drive over to the Everetts'.

But as I round the curve of the drive, the landscape looks strangely unfamiliar. It takes me a couple of shocked seconds to register that one of the tall oaks has been blown over and is now completely blocking my exit. So I'm stuck. Completely and utterly cut off. And completely and utterly alone. I put my head on my arms on the steering wheel and allow the helpless, angry tears of frustration, exhaustion and despair to escape.

After a couple of minutes of wallowing in self-pity, I realise that this isn't going to help in any way whatsoever. I pull myself together with effort and wipe my eyes. Suddenly I notice that rescue is at hand. Making her way purposefully along the lane is a little old lady in a familiar black dress and now she's waving reassuringly at me and shouting something I can't quite hear.

With a surge of relief and gratitude I jump out of the car and clamber over the tangled branches of the fallen tree to hug Mireille, my saviour.

When I lead her onto the terrace, she tuts sympathetically at the scene of devastation before her. "My dear girl, it's so lucky you weren't hurt. Now don't worry about a thing. The electricity will be back on soon. They're used to these storms around here and I saw the EDF van going past a few minutes ago."

I sigh deeply. "Well, once the phones are back on I suppose I'll have to call Monsieur Dubois and ask him for his brother-in-law's number so I can get him to come round and mend the roof."

"Pah," retorts Mireille with utter scorn, "that philandering Parisian. You're not having any of them to do the work. No, you have the perfect work force much closer at hand. Don't you know my sons are stonemasons? They'll come round and sort all this out for you. And I'll tell Raphael to bring the chainsaw too, so they can clear your driveway before they do anything else."

Weak-kneed with relief, I sit down on the terrace wall. "Oh Mireille, I'd be so grateful. But it's the weekend. I can probably manage until Monday if they wouldn't mind coming then."

"Weekend nothing! In an emergency we all lend a hand to help our neighbours in the country you know. They'll be here this afternoon. I'm the boss!" And with a final reassuring pat on my tousled head she sweeps regally back up the lane to mobilise her troops.

*

At precisely two o'clock I hear the purposeful hum of a distant chainsaw at the foot of the drive. Mireille taps at the kitchen door. "They're just clearing the tree so they can get the truck through. Have you got your power back on? Good. They'll leave the tree lying in the grass. You'll have a good supply of wood for the fire, but oak is tough so it needs to season for a year before you can cut it up. At least it'll be out of your way though. Ah, here they come now."

A large white truck rumbles ponderously up the drive and sways to a halt in the courtyard, dwarfing my little car. On the side is stencilled neatly 'Thibault Frères, Maçonnerie' and a local phone number. Two smiling men jump out and are followed by two more on foot, one of them carrying a large orange chainsaw. All four are wearing neat green overalls and they line up respectfully before their mother, towering above her, awaiting her instructions.

"Mademoiselle Gina, these are my sons," she says with a hint of maternal pride. "Raphael, Florian, Cédric and Pierre."

Each in turn reaches to shake my hand. The first three have warm, dark eyes the colour of molasses and neat brush-cut hair, graded from salt-and-pepper (Raphael), through greying-at-the-temples (Florian) to pure black (Cédric). The fourth, Pierre, who appears to be in his early twenties and a good dozen years younger than the others, has an unruly mop of dark curls and blue eyes that sparkle with self-confident charm.

"It's a great pleasure to meet you," I say. "And thank you for coming to help me so quickly." I repeat each of their names in turn to make sure I've got them right. Fleetingly I wonder what Liz would make of the flowery names of the elder three.

"Pierre?" I say with a smile, as a thought occurs to me. It reminds me of those old jokes – what do you call a man with a seagull on his head? Cliff. A stonemason called Pierre is like a miner called Doug. Or a gardener called Flora. Or a DJ called Mike, (although come to think of it I'm sure there've been quite a few of those). It's obviously a well-worn joke, as Pierre rolls his eyes and his three brothers grin.

"Yes, I know," sighs Mireille. "My dear departed husband, may God rest his soul, was a stonemason. When his first son was born he wanted to call him Pierre. But I had other ideas. It was the same with Florian and Cédric. Finally, when we knew another baby was on the way, twelve years after Cédric, I was absolutely sure it was going to be a girl this time. So to keep my husband happy I said if it was a boy we could call him Pierre. And so here he is."

"Although some would say he is a bit of a girl with this head of hair," teases Florian ruffling his baby brother's head to annoy him.

"Ah, you're just jealous because I'm so popular with the women," shrugs Pierre. Cédric rolls his eyes in mock despair and grins at me and I notice that around his smiling eyes is an etching of finely chiselled lines that seem to tell a story of something else: weariness or sadness or pain? Whatever it is, it runs beneath the surface like a deeply-buried fault line through bedrock.

"That's enough, boys," says their mother firmly. "Come and see what needs to be done round the other side of the house." She and I lead the way. The four men take the scene of devastation completely in their stride and quickly set to work, each with his own set tasks.

"Don't worry Gina, they'll soon have this put right. At the very least you'll have the hole in the roof patched up before nightfall," says Mireille comfortingly.

"It's going to take us a bit longer to rebuild the chimney I'm afraid," says Raphael.

They are putting up a scaffolding tower beside the house and Cédric is surveying the roof from the top of a tall ladder alongside it."There's quite a bit of damage to the tiles up here," he calls down. "Really the whole roof needs to be re-done. Some of these joists look like they need replacing completely."

With dismay I think of my redundancy money which won't go far if it has to pay for a whole new roof. I wonder what the insurance will cover. Seeing the look on my face, Mireille says, "Well, just patch it up as best you can for now. If Gina decides she wants the whole thing done later you can always come back." She turns to me. "I'm going to leave you now. Nathalie and her brother Luc are at my house for the afternoon so I'd better get back. Just ask the boys if you have any questions or need any help."

I hug her and thank her profusely for saving me.

"Nonsense, that's what neighbours are for," she replies.

A couple of hours later I stick my head out of the French windows."Would anyone like a cup of tea?" I ask.

"Non merci," reply Raphael and Florian, with looks of alarm at the thought of this strange foreign idea. But Cédric says, "Please, I'd like to try one," and Pierre says, "A coffee would be good for me," so I busy myself setting things out on a tray.

"It's so kind of you, coming to help me out on a Saturday," I say as the two brothers pause to drink.

"It's no problem," smiles Cédric kindly, gingerly sipping a cup of black tea. "We'll fix things up temporarily today and come back next week to finish the job properly." The floral mug looks delicate in his large, capable hand.

Pierre, meanwhile, has knocked back his coffee in a single gulp and is busily consulting the mobile phone he's fished out of a pocket of his overalls.

"Aha," says Cédric, "Pierre is busy fixing up his social life for this evening. He's usually spoilt for choice on a Saturday night."

Contemplating my own blank agenda, I mean to express the fact that I'm envious of Pierre's dilemma. "*Ah, j'ai envie de toi*," I say. And then, given the look of surprise on the faces of both men, I realise I've just come out with one of those awful linguistic mistakes that still ambush me now and then, even though I definitely should know better.

Cédric throws back his head and guffaws. "Mademoiselle Gina, I think you mean to say '*je t'envie*'!"

Oh god, I feel myself blushing to the roots of my hair as it dawns on me that I've just told Mireille's youngest son that I desire him.

Pierre, in the meantime, has regained his composure and replies, "Well perhaps she does mean what she says. It's a common reaction amongst women when they first meet me, after all."

Cédric gives him a mock cuff around the ear. "Insufferable brat," he says fondly. "Just ignore him," he tells me.

In confusion, I collect up our cups and scurry back inside, blushing again as I hear Pierre recounting my mistake to his two elder brothers on the roof who both whoop with laughter.

By five-thirty they've patched the hole in the roof with plastic sheeting and have made a neat stack of unbroken roof tiles, clearing away the shattered debris. "If they're not in your way, we'll leave our tools here until Monday," says Raphael and I assure him I'm not planning on carrying out any major terrace renovations myself this weekend. They take their leave and the truck swings off up the drive, Raphael and Florian in the front and the two younger men perched in the back.

I follow on foot to go and check whether there's any post in the mail box on the lane. I reach into the metal box and pull out a large envelope with a coloured crest and 'Institute of Masters of Wine' inscribed in one corner. Oh good, it must be the application forms I asked for.

I look up as I hear a roar in the lane and a cavalcade of vehicles pulls out of Mireille's gate. First comes a helmeted figure on a red motorbike who sweeps by with a jaunty wave – Pierre, I surmise, heading off for his Saturday night social whirl. Next a stately green Volvo sails by and Raphael gives me a grave salute. Then the white truck comes past and

Florian waves at me cheerfully. And finally a practical-looking dark blue pickup comes along the lane with Cédric at the wheel. Next to him is a young boy with the same dark hair and eyes as his father. And from the narrow back seat a serious, heart-shaped face framed with long dark hair gazes out. They pull up alongside and Nathalie winds down her window. "Bonjour Mademoiselle Gina. Was Lafite alright in the storm? I hope he wasn't too frightened."

"Hello Nathalie. Don't worry, he's fine. He didn't like getting his fur wet much though."

"Give him a stroke from me," she replies.

"I will. You'll have to come and see him one day soon. He's missing you."

The little girl smiles and Cédric pulls off with a wave. I stand by the post-box watching them disappear up the road.

And am surprised to note that I feel a distinct pang of disappointment that Nathalie and Luc belong to Cédric, and not to Florian or Raphael.

*

I'm determined not to be beaten by my disastrous first attempt at painting and decorating. I put on my cut-off shorts and a vest top which has definitely seen better days, and stand, hands on hips, surveying the scabrous, flaking shutters. Sunday is cranking itself up to be another baking hot day and so at least the soft old wood has dried out now. The peeling patches of paint are worse than ever though and there's no doubt it all needs to be removed somehow. I'm sure I saw some sheets of sandpaper in a drawer in the kitchen during my frantic cleaning frenzy and I go in search of them and also my iPod, which I tuck into the back pocket of my shorts, fixing the earphones into my ears. A little energising music is just what I need for this job.

Now, we might as well get this out into the open right now. I freely confess my taste in music is not always the coolest. Don't get me wrong, I often listen to classical music and have a modest but widely-ranging collection, from Albinoni to Vaughan Williams. I also have a lot of modern stuff by really street-cred groups like U2 and The Red Hot Chilli Peppers, which is the sort of thing I readily admit to when having those conversations with friends that start, "So what do you have on your iPod then?" But stashed away beneath the respectable surface of such socially-acceptable works is my shameful secret library. Meat Loaf, Cher and Bonny Tyler rub shoulders with Kirsty MacColl, The Bangles and The Dixie Chicks. Bryan Adams and Enrique Iglesias compete with Take That and Boyzone for my attention. And Plastic Bertrand and Johhny Hallyday add a little culture in French – if culture is the right word, which it probably isn't.

Oh come on, there's a time and a place for Mozart and sanding shutters definitely isn't it. And anyway, let he or she who is entirely without an

Abba number tucked away somewhere in their collection throw the first stone.

So now I select an appropriately upbeat playlist, crank up the volume and set to with the sandpaper. The paint, both old and new, comes off with gratifying ease. It's good exercise too, especially if you add a few dance moves while you work, although the stepladder does tend to wobble a bit. My spirits lift as a new, smoothly uniform surface of freshly sanded wood is exposed and I start to sing.

I'm just explaining to my reflection in the window that 'I'm holding out for a hero 'til the morning light, and he's got to be fast and he's got to be strong...' and I'm giving it some of my very best moves when I suddenly realise that, just like in the song, there really is somebody out there watching me.

Luckily he's close enough to put a steadying hand on the stepladder as I jump so hard it lurches alarmingly. I look down from my precarious perch into the warm, laughing eyes of Cédric.

Wrenching the earphones from my ears, I scramble down to firmer ground, my neck and cheeks blazing scarlet with embarrassment. "Excuse me, I was just..." I burble, waving a dusty hand at the shutters. My shoulders and arms are covered in freckles of dried green and red paint. And it's only later that I discover the bits in my hair as well.

Why is it that whenever I'm wearing my most scruffy and revealing clothes, an unexpected

Frenchman comes sailing up the drive? Perhaps there's a whole posse of them lurking in the bushes watching and then the minute I put on an outfit that I'd prefer not to be seen dead in, they send another one along to ensure maximum mortification. I can just imagine Monsieur Dubois nudging Cédric, "Go on, I did it last time. Your turn next..."

And exactly how long has he been standing there? I cast my mind back to the previous song on the playlist. Omigod, did he get here in time to catch my ladder-top rendition of 'There's a guy works down the chip shop swears he's Elvis'?

Cédric gallantly pretends he hasn't noticed that I'm not really wearing many clothes, nor that he's witnessed any of my grand command performance up the ladder. Composing his features into an expression of professional gravity, (though that irrepressible twinkle in his eyes speaks volumes), he shakes my grubby hand.

"Bonjour Mademoiselle Gina. Please forgive me for disturbing you. I just wanted to pick up one or two of the tools we left here yesterday. My mother lost a couple of roof tiles in the storm and I'm fixing them for her." He nods at the shutters. "You're doing a good job there," he says chivalrously, choosing to ignore the fact that I've clearly bodged things terribly on my first attempt.

"However," he continues solicitously, "if you would allow me to make a suggestion, you might find it easier to take the shutters down before you sand them. You'll find it a bit more stable on solid ground," he can't resist adding with a grin.

I attempt to regain my composure, concentrating on the shutters with what I hope appears to be an air of competent efficiency. "Why yes, of course, they're just a little heavy for me to take down on my own."

And in fact it hadn't even occurred to me that this might be a possibility, but on closer inspection it looks like they'll simply lift off their hinges quite easily.

In the space of a couple of minutes, Cédric has taken the shutters off all the windows and piled them in a neat stack on the grass. "I believe your aunt had a pair of trestles in the shed," he says, leading the way.

So that's what those wooden frames are – I did wonder.

"You'll be wanting to put a good primer on them after you've finished the sanding. Mr Bricolage has ones for exterior woodwork. Look for one marked for extreme conditions. The weather here can be pretty wild as you've already discovered."

Ah, so that's where I went wrong. Primer.

"Yes, of course, I was intending getting just that," I say.

"The large shutters on the doors are very heavy," he continues. "But you have enough to be getting on with here and then tomorrow, when my brothers and I return, we'll lift the others off for you."

As he finishes speaking, there's the sound of car tyres coming up the drive and we both turn to see who it is. 'Great,' I think, 'someone else dropping by, just to ensure my humiliation is complete.'

My heart sinks still further as Nigel Yates pulls up beside us and jumps out. He comes round the side of the car and embraces me like a long-lost friend. "My dear Gina," he exclaims, ignoring Cédric. "I heard you'd had some damage in that awful storm the other night. Thought I'd come to the rescue!"

Heard how, I wonder fleetingly, the power of the bush telegraph in a small rural community still a novelty to me.

"Cédric Thibault, Nigel Yates," I make the introductions so he has to turn to acknowledge Cédric, who is standing by patiently with a polite smile on his face.

"Monsieur," Nigel says with a curt nod.

"Cédric and his brothers are stonemasons. They very kindly came yesterday to patch up the worst of the damage and are coming back tomorrow to carry on with the job. So it's good of you to come by, but thanks to the Thibaults everything's under control."

Instead of sharing my delight at this fortunate turn of events, Nigel appears somewhat annoyed. He spots the pile of shutters. "And are they fixing shutters for you too?" he asks.

"Non," replies Cédric, who has clearly understood the gist of our conversation, "Mademioselle Gina is undertaking that work herself. I was just giving her a hand taking the shutters down. In fact, now that you're here perhaps we can remove the larger ones too."

"Of course," replies Nigel, in a tone that suggests he is man enough for any such challenge, and he removes his jacket, arranging it somewhat fussily across the back seat of his car. I can't help but compare the slight flabbiness of his stomach beneath his neatly tucked-in shirt with the firm muscularity of Cédric's midriff under his clean white t-shirt.

Leading the way, Nigel seizes the first large shutter beside the front door and heaves it upwards but it doesn't budge. Cédric produces a hammer and chisel and, with a few deft taps, loosens the hinges. Taking a side each, the men lift the heavy wooden panel and carry it over to lean it against a tree beside the trestles. They repeat the exercise until all the door shutters have been removed, by which time Nigel's face is looking distinctly red and shiny and the long, carefully arranged strands of hair covering his receding hairline have flopped free and are hanging down, in a somewhat alarming style, over one ear. Damp stains have appeared under the sleeves of his shirt, the tail of which has come adrift from his waistband.

Although, of course, I'm hardly in a position to criticise, given my own scruffy state.

Cédric, on the other hand, remains neatly unruffled and hardly seems to have exerted himself at all in lifting the heavy and cumbersome shutters.

When they've finished there's an awkward pause. "Would anyone like a glass of water?" I ask, to fill it.

Nigel accepts with alacrity, combing his hair with his fingers to plaster the wayward locks back into position.

"Non merci," says Cédric. "I must get on with fixing my mother's roof." He picks up a box of tools. "See you tomorrow Gina," he says, shaking my hand, "and *bonne continuation* with your work. Monsieur," he nods and politely proffers a hand to Nigel.

Once Cédric disappears down the drive, Nigel turns to me. "You want to be careful about who you use to do work on your house you know Gina. You can't just ask the first cowboy who comes along. And French workmen can be tricky. I've got an excellent English builder who I use. I'll phone him for you first thing tomorrow and ask him to come by and look at what needs doing."

"Thank you, but that won't be necessary," I say firmly, trying not to let my annoyance show. "The Thibault brothers are extremely experienced and I'm lucky to have them."

"But it's tricky communicating – presumably they don't speak any English, so how will you tell them what you want done?"

"That won't be a problem," I reply shortly. "I speak excellent French."

As long as you ignore the occasional complete foot-in-mouth bloomer, I think. And also the fact that I haven't the first clue about roof construction in English, never mind in French, so I have no idea what I want done. Other than the fact that I want it all put back to how it was. And preferably so that it won't blow down again in the next storm either.

Nigel is clearly not picking up, from the warning note in my voice, the fact that he's seriously beginning to piss me off. "Well, I just hope they're not ripping you off," he persists. "What's their quote for the job? They tend to have one price for the French and one for the English you know."

I don't want to admit to him that I haven't had a quote, that in fact I haven't asked at all what this is going to cost. "They're giving me an excellent price and I'm more than satisfied that they'll do a good job. They come very highly recommended."

By their own mother, admittedly.

"Thank you for your offer of help, but I've got it all under control," I end firmly. "Now, if you've finished your water, please excuse me. I must get back to my sanding."

I hold out a hand to take the glass from him.

"Well, I'll be interested to see how you get on. Let me know if you have any problems with the work. I just hope they get it finished before they bugger off on holiday for most of August. The French do you know. Remember, I'm always here if you need anything. Us ex-pats have to stick together!" And with a slightly damp peck on each cheek, he finally departs.

"Yuk," I say, rubbing my face and watching his car disappear. "I'm not bloody sticking anything anywhere with you, that's for sure." And with renewed energy I plug myself back in to my iPod, turning the volume up high again, and take my irritation out on the next shutter.

Chapter 8.

By the end of the following week things are feeling far more under control.

Hugh and Celia have come for an evening drink and we sit on the terrace with a bottle of *blanc sec* on the table before us, condensation forming a thirst-quenching dew on the glasses before us, even before we take the first sip.

I love these blended Bordeaux whites. The mixture of crisply angular Sauvignon Blanc and softer, rounder Sémillon makes for a subtle complexity in the best examples of their kind. I never tire of blends the way I sometimes do of single *cépage* wines. Chardonnay for instance, which was so trendy in the early nineties, before people started to realise that the flabby, heavily-oaked New World version was, in fact, neither particularly drinkable nor particularly pleasant.

Celia raises her glass. "Cheers Gina. You've had quite a fortnight for your first two weeks in France! But you seem to have coped admirably and I'm sure it can only get better."

I lift my glass in return and take the first sip of my cool wine, savouring the balance and depth of the flavour. It's as good as when I first tasted it at the little local château just down the road.

If only you knew, I think. The roof has been an almost welcome diversion from the discovery that my father had a secret, passionate affair with his sister-in-law at some point in his married life. And, for all I know, it may have continued until he died. I wonder how I can bring the conversation round to the subject of my father nonchalantly, to see whether the Everetts know anything about the timing and frequency of his possible visits here.

But Hugh's more interested in the progress of my roof than in idle chit-chat. He tips his head back to look up at the scaffolding which still encases the wall of the house.

"You know Gina, you were terribly lucky getting the Thibault brothers, and at such short notice. They're the best in the area, real craftsmen. Everyone wants them for their building projects. There's usually a six-month wait. You've obviously charmed them," he smiles archly.

"Hm, I think it was more the fact that their mother ordered them to do it than anything to do with me," I reply. "I'm very lucky to have a neighbour who wields so much clout."

"Poor you though," chips in Celia. "All that added expense and on something as boring as a roof."

"Yes, boring but rather essential, as I rapidly realised once I didn't actually have one anymore. But I've been incredibly lucky there too. The insurance assessor came straight round when I called him after the storm and they're going to cover quite a bit of the cost. The Thibaults have given me a very reasonable price for the rest of the job, so thankfully it's not going to make too much of a dent in my redundancy money."

Hugh looks at the roof appraisingly. "Looks like they've replaced the tiles over a very large area though. That's quite a significant amount of work. Their mother's clout obviously extends to the brothers' billing philosophy too. You really do have friends in high places, if you'll forgive the pun," he smiles, with a nod at the scaffolding.

"Well, all's well that ends well," says Celia. "Looks like you've been busy yourself too. The shutters are looking very elegant. I do like the colour you've chosen. But look at your poor hands!" She grabs my spare hand, the one not holding a wine glass, to inspect.

"I know," I sigh. "My fingernails are a thing of the past. And the primer is very hard to get off." I point out the rims of white which stubbornly refuse to come off around my roughened cuticles. "Still, it's very satisfying and it's been keeping me busy. I've just got a few more to do. No doubt the pace of work will slow down a bit now though. I got my internet connection up and running today."

"Well, you've certainly achieved a great deal in the short time you've been here. Bravo!" Celia congratulates me. "Now then," she continues, "it's time you took a break from all this and had a bit of a social life instead. Next Tuesday's the 14th you know. Bastille Day. We're making up a big table at the festivities in Gensac and we'd love it if you could come along. It's great fun. They put up long trestle tables in the *place* and there's a meal. Everyone brings their own plates and cutlery and you can buy bottles of wine from local producers. Afterwards there are fireworks and dancing. Do come, it's quite the social event of the year."

It does sound fun and suddenly I realise that it would be nice to have a break from my own company for an evening.

"That would be lovely," I say.

"Well, come to us first. You can leave the car and we'll walk into the village together," Celia beams.

"Delighted you can join us," says Hugh. "I hope you'll save the first dance for me." He raises his glass for another sip. "Now, tell us all about this Master of Wine course you're going to be doing."

A while later, as they get up to go, Hugh turns to me as if something's just occurred to him and says casually – a shade too casually perhaps - "By the way Gina, the funeral parlour asked me to pick up Liz's ashes a few days ago. We've got the urn safely back at our house, but I don't know what you were planning to do with them? That's one point Liz didn't cover in her will. We'll be happy to hang on to them for as long as you like. No rush. Just thought you should know that they're there whenever you decide you want them."

I'm a bit taken aback. I'd completely forgotten about them. And what on earth do I want to do with them now?

"OK, thanks Hugh," I say briskly. "I'll have a think and let you know."

So that's another sleepless night as I toss and turn in the bed in the spare room, to where I decamped after the storm, wondering what the right thing to do would be with the final bodily remains of my favourite aunt. My mother's sister. My friend.

My father's mistress.

*

I'm up early the next morning and head down to Sainte Foy for the Saturday market. Liz always used to say, "You have to get there before all the English appear if you want the best produce. Fortunately, though, they only manage to get themselves out of bed by about eleven o'clock so it's only the last hour that's a complete scrum."

I love browsing at the hundreds of stalls that line the narrow streets of the old *bastide* town. There's certainly a variety, with everything from cheap clothes and tacky knock-off jewellery to delicious local produce and pretty arts-and-crafts. I'm standing in the queue at my favourite fruit stall, waiting to buy some of the mouth-wateringly juicy yellow nectarines that have just come into season, when I feel a small tug at my sleeve.

I turn to find Nathalie in the queue behind me.

"*Bonjour Mademoiselle Gina,*" she says, and I bend to plant the customary two kisses on her upturned face.

The attractive woman beside her extends a hand in greeting. "*Bonjour Mademoiselle Peplow.* I am Marie-Louise Thibault. I've heard a lot about you. Pleased to meet you. I hope the work on your roof hasn't been too disruptive for you?"

So this must be Cédric's wife. She has a cloud of dark curly hair and is wearing slim jeans and a crisp white shirt. She looks effortlessly and understatedly sexy in the way that only certain Frenchwomen can.

A line from an Alanis Morisette song sounds unbidden in my head. Isn't it, indeed, ironic?

Her hand is soft and immaculately manicured, and I am uncomfortably conscious of my own leathery palms and tattered, broken nails as I take it in mine. Her handshake is firmly friendly.

I assure Marie-Louise that the work is progressing well. "I'm very grateful to your husband and his brothers for getting it done so quickly."

"Yes, it's lucky. I think they said they should just be able to get it finished before we go on holiday. We're off to the *bassin* at Arcachon in a week's time, you know, aren't we Nathalie."

I didn't know. I feel a pang of disappointment that the job will be finished so soon. I've enjoyed

116

having the brothers around this week, their banter and laughter in the background a companionable accompaniment to my painting duties on the other side of the house.

And I shall miss the afternoon tea-breaks, which have become a daily occurrence, with Pierre and Cédric. Most of all Cédric, I think. And then briskly dismiss the thought, before Marie-Louise can read my guilty mind.

"*Oui*, I'm really looking forward to swimming," Nathalie chimes in. "But even more. I'm looking forward to Tuesday evening. It's Bastille Day you know, Mademoiselle Gina. We're going to buy me a new dress after we've finished shopping here."

Marie-Louise smoothes the little girl's fine, dark hair, a gesture that is so full of love it makes my throat ache. "We are indeed. Because you've grown so much in the last few months and nothing fits." She smiles at me.

"Well, I am going to be there too, so I'll look forward to seeing you," I say.

"Good," says Nathalie, "it's such fun." Then she looks momentarily worried. "But you must shut Lafite inside. He won't like it if he hears the fireworks you know. They'll scare him."

"Don't worry," I reassure her. "I'll leave him some extra food and put on some soothing music that he likes, so he won't hear the bangs."

"Good idea," nods the little girl solemnly.

Marie-Louise touches my arm lightly. The gold of the wedding ring on her left hand winks cheerfully – mockingly it seems to me – in the sunshine. "It's your turn now, Mademoiselle," she nods towards the stallholder.

My nectarines safely stashed in my basket, I turn to say goodbye, but Marie-Louise is already engaged in conversation with the lady behind the stall. Nathalie gives me a little wave.

"See you on Tuesday," I say, and allow myself to be swept up by the strengthening current of the market throng. So that I don't have to dwell on the fact that this encounter has reminded me I am still very much an outsider here.

*

I'm standing in front of the wardrobe in the spare room, dispassionately regarding my reflection in the soft, freckled silver of the mirror which is misty with age around the edges. Despite copious slatherings of Factor 20 sunscreen my skin has turned a rich golden brown from hours spent sanding and painting in the hot July sun. My hair, usually a rather boring mouse colour, now has expensive-looking highlights of streaky blonde, also courtesy of the sun's bleaching rays. I've had a long lukewarm bath, soaking and scrubbing away the dust and paint spots, and have treated my thirsty skin to the last precious drops of my Jo Malone body lotion. And I've put on and taken off at least a dozen different outfits which are now deposited in muddled heaps on the bed.

Bastille Night and I haven't got a thing to wear.

'Oh come on,' I tell my reflection somewhat testily. 'Don't be ridiculous, woman. It's a casual local gathering, not Queen Charlotte's Ball.' (Does Queen Charlotte's Ball still exist these days, I wonder. Roddy would know. But that has nothing to do with my current dilemma and actually, now I come to think of it, I couldn't care less about either Roddy or balls. His own or the ones you dance at.)

With a sigh, I pick up a black summer dress and pull it over my head for the second time in ten minutes. It's not right, much too formal, and besides the only shoes that go with it are a pair of high-heeled sandals that spell a guaranteed sprained ankle, at the very least, when dancing on the stones of Gensac's pretty *place*. I peel off the dress again and wrench open the wardrobe door. The Ossie Clark tunic gleams seductively on its hanger. I've purposely been avoiding it, even though it's the one thing I really want to wear and I know it would be perfect for this evening. But it would feel like a betrayal to wear anything of Liz's.

Maybe she even wore it when she was with my father. I push the thought out of my head.

I rifle through the other clothes left in the wardrobe, in the vain hope that something else will leap out at me as being the perfect solution to my sartorial dilemma. But any possibilities have already been taken out, tried on and discarded on the bed. Methodically, I return each of them to their hangers and put them back where they belong. I glance at my watch, which tells me time has now run out. And then quickly, so I won't think about it anymore, I pull on a pair of flowing linen trousers, wrench the vintage top down from the rail and slip it over my head. As the cool silk drapes itself against my tanned skin, I know that, conscience or no conscience, this is what I'm wearing.

Anyway she probably never did wear it with Dad. And if she did that has nothing to do with here and now. So there.

I buckle on a pair of strappy gladiator sandals and give my hair a final comb before going through to the kitchen. We're far enough away from both Gensac and Sainte Foy that I doubt the noise of the fireworks will be anything more than a series of very muffled pops at the most, but a sudden vision of Nathalie's serious little face makes me pour some extra food into Lafite's bowl and turn on some soothing music. Attracted by the sound of the food pattering into his bowl, rather than Kiri Te Kanawa's singing I suspect, the old cat appears and rubs himself fondly against my ankle. "Now you're staying in tonight and I, for once, am going out," I tell him, gently stroking his furry cheek. I leave him happily munching, pick up a basket containing my plate, cutlery and glass for the meal and lock the door behind me.

The narrow streets of Gensac are abuzz with people hurrying in the same direction towards the open square in the middle of the village, all carrying cheerily clinking bags and baskets. Strings of red, white and blue bunting overhead mark the way and above them swifts dart and soar in the opal sky as if sharing the excitement of the chattering crowd below. Hugh, Celia and I join the gathering throng and, turning the corner, pause to take in the scene in the *place* before us.

The square has been transformed from its daytime serenity into a humming party venue. Long trestle tables are arranged before us and groups of people are gathering round each one, chattering and embracing as they greet one another and then set out their glasses and cutlery on the white paper table covers. Under the soaring plane tree that dominates the heart of the village a wooden dance floor has been laid out and the Mayor begins testing the public address system, through a microphone somewhat reluctantly handed over by the DJ from behind the flashing facade of his disco. Red and white streamers radiate from the tree to form a fluttering canopy above our heads, and golden fairy lights are just starting to gleam as the dusk deepens. And in and out of everything small children dart and race, unwittingly mirroring the flight of the swifts high above us all.

We hand over a few Euros in exchange for strips of tickets that entitle us to each of the four courses of tonight's meal. Celia cranes her neck and then waves. "There are the others. I told them to bag a table if they got here before us."

We pick our way between the tables to join the rest of our party, who are already well-established by the look of the open bottles of wine arranged the length of the table. Celia pretends not to notice as Nigel, looking as rosily damp as ever, waves me over, gesticulating at the empty space on the bench beside him. "Gina, I've saved you a seat!" He clambers to his feet and embraces me somewhat stickily. There's nothing for it but to sit down next to him, but I'm relieved to notice that the Everetts take up their places across from us and Hugh gives me a reassuring wink as he settles himself at the table.

"Let me pour you some wine," says Nigel, enthusiastically sloshing some of the local co-op's finest (which isn't at all bad actually) into my glass.

"Just a half, thanks, I'm driving," I say, firmly putting my hand over the top. I've taken the precaution of including a large bottle of water in my basket and I place this on the table between us, signalling my clear intention not to succumb to any further temptations he may try to put my way.

Hugh introduces me to the large lady sitting on the other side of me and, to my relief, she engages me in an animated conversation about the forthcoming Franco-British week in Sainte Foy which apparently includes a French versus English *boules* tournament in which she is very keen that I should participate.

Above the crowd's noisy crescendo, the loudspeakers on either side of the disco give a sudden shriek of feedback and the Mayor declares the proceedings officially open with a hearty welcome, inviting us to take our plates and make our way to the serving tables at the top of the *place* where we will be given our starters.

Despite the hordes of people, the queues move surprisingly quickly, the servers obviously long-practised in their efficiency in doling out slices of charcuterie and hunks of crusty bread onto each outstretched plate in turn. And besides, the queues are a further opportunity to mingle, greet more friends and exchange gossip as the tide of partygoers swirls and eddies between the tables.

"So how's your roof coming on?" asks Nigel, returning to his seat close on my heels and tucking in to the array of garlic-spiked pâté and cold meats on the plate before him.

"Very well indeed, thank you," I retort, trying to keep the edge of irritation and defensiveness out of my voice. "The Thibaults are doing an excellent job. They'll have the outside pretty much done by the end of the week. Then they're off on holiday for a fortnight. They'll only be back to finish off and re-plaster the ceiling in August but there's no great hurry for that."

"Typical French workmen," he sniffs. "It's impossible to get anything done at all in the summer. You'll be lucky if you see them again before September. I'm surprised they're doing the plastering. Surely you need a proper plasterer for that? Mind you, they're impossible to come by. Expensive work too. Let me know if you want one who speaks English. I can ask my builder for you if you like."

"Thank you, but I have every confidence in the Thibaults and I'm sure they'll be back to finish the job. Their mother is a neighbour of mine and she'll chase them up for me if need be." I've got a sneaking suspicion that they're doing the plastering themselves to keep costs down for me, but I'm not going to share this thought with Nigel.

I take a sip of the rough red wine, pausing to enjoy the way the robustly tannic local brew compliments the fattiness of the spicy charcuterie.

Across the square at another of the long tables, I spot Mireille and her family. All four sons are there and I see Luc and Nathalie sitting between Cédric and Marie-Louise, happily tucking into their meal, surrounded by assorted aunts and cousins. Their diminutive grandmother holds court at one end of the long wooden bench, pausing frequently over her starter to greet a constant stream of friends and neighbours who come up to say hello.

Celia leans across the table, following my gaze. "Isn't that Madame Thibault?" she asks. "We must go and say hello later on. And that tall lady on the next table along is our local novelist, Abigail Peters. Have you read any of her books? Quite a celebrity in these parts." She pauses to scan the square for other noteworthy characters. "You see the woman on the next table but one? The one that looks a bit like Carla Bruni? Well she's a ballet dancer from Paris. She and her husband have bought a wreck of a château and are doing it up. That's him at this end of the table – rather dishy."

She breaks off to half-rise and greet Monsieur le Maire who is doing the rounds of the tables, encouraging people to make their way back to the serving tables with their empty plates to collect the main course. He shakes my hand and pronounces himself to be "*enchanté*" to make my acquaintance.

"Shall we...?" says Nigel, picking up his plate and sliding off the bench to allow me to go first. We file up to join the queues once again. As I stand in the line I feel a gentle tug on my sleeve and turn round to find Cédric and Nathalie behind me, also with their plates in their hands. "*Bonsoir* Mademoiselle Gina," says Nathalie who is still holding the silky sleeve of my tunic. I bend to kiss her on each cheek. "I like your outfit," she says shyly. "Papa, doesn't she look elegant?"

"She does indeed," smiles Cédric gallantly. And then, to my surprise, he also leans to kiss me twice and I feel myself blushing involuntarily where his slightly rough cheek has brushed mine.

To cover my confusion, I bend back towards Nathalie. "And you look absolutely beautiful," I say. "Is that your new dress? It's so pretty."

The little girl beams. "*Oui*, pink is my favourite colour," she replies. "And how is Lafite? Did you shut him in safely?"

"Yes, I left him listening to a little Mozart so I think he'll be fine."

Nigel, who's been chatting to some of the other members of our party, turns towards me and, to my intense annoyance, puts a proprietorial – and somewhat clammy – hand on the small of my back to usher me forward. "Here you go Gina, it's our turn next."

I smile again at Nathalie and Cédric. "Would you like to go first?" I offer.

"That's very kind, but we'll wait for the rest of the family," says Cédric and I see that Luc, Marie-Louise and the others are getting up from their table. "*Bonsoir* Monsieur," he adds politely to Nigel, who gives him a rather curt nod in reply.

"OK. Well, *bonne continuation*," I say.

As I make my way back to the table, my plate piled high with chicken and rice, I make a small detour to say hello to Mireille who has now joined the queue with the rest of her family. I kiss her, Marie-Louise and Luc and greet the brothers, including Pierre who juggles mobile phone and plate to shake my hand. But then I move on swiftly so I won't hold them up in getting their meal. They are in the middle of a noisy, merry throng of friends and I'm an outsider here. And besides, my food's getting cold.

The cheerful cacophony of clinking glasses, clattering cutlery and chattering voices grows louder than ever as the meal nears its end, cheeses and choc ices following the main course. Finally the Mayor and his band of helpers circulate with bin bags to collect debris and plates are scraped thoroughly before being stowed carefully back into bags and baskets, the decks cleared for the evening's main events. Darkness has now fallen and the fairy lights sparkle merrily beneath their canopy of paper streamers, replicated above several million-fold by the Milky Way. The DJ takes his place behind the bank of flashing lights and suddenly music floods the square and there's a tidal surge towards the dance floor as couples begin to spin and sway to a Johnny Hallyday number. Small boys, fuelled up on ice-cream and excitement now, race in and out of the dancers and groups of little girls, in pretty dresses with their hair tied up in jaunty red, white and blue bows, hop solemnly and a little self-consciously on the edge of the bobbing, spinning throng.

I'm chatting to Hugh and some of the others sitting around the table whose white paper cover is now festively printed with silver grease spots and pink circles of wine, when suddenly I'm aware that Nigel is trying hard to attract my attention. He's drunk most of his bottle of wine and it hasn't done much to enhance his charms. His face is now flushed a deep shade of magenta, clashing violently with his pink shirt, and his features, framed by their strands of sweat-slicked hair, have slackened and sagged. I studiously try to ignore this beguiling apparition bobbing increasingly persistently on the periphery of my vision. But then he puts a sticky hand on my upper arm, leaving a damp paw-print on the silk of my sleeve.

Hugh, seeing my plight, leaps to his feet with alacrity and reaches a hand across the table. "Now Gina, I believe we have a date for the first dance," he says. "Nigel, if you'll excuse us?"

He leads me to the dance floor.

"Thank you, that was kind," I say.

"Probably just a stay of execution I'm afraid," he grins. "Don't think you're going to get away without a dance with him. But we can at least show him how it's done."

To my surprise, Hugh commences an accomplished jive, leading me so that I quickly pick up the steps and am soon happily hopping and twirling. "This is fun!" I shriek, as he whisks me round the dance floor. "Where did you learn to dance like this?"

"On our five-year posting to Senegal there wasn't much else to do. The ex-pats, mostly French, ran Ceroc classes and Celia and I signed up. We even won the dance-off at the Christmas party one year.

First prize, a bottle of the local hooch. Second prize, two bottles of the local hooch."

He steers me deftly round another bobbing couple.

"Shame your mother isn't here for the party. Will she be coming to visit you soon?"

"No plans," I shout above the beat of the music, as our orbit has now brought us alongside one of the banks of speakers that flank the disco's flashing lights.

"It's a pity she couldn't come more often when your father used to be over on his tasting trips, but I suppose she was quite tied at home then, with you at school and so on."

I miss a turn and stumble clumsily.

"Whoops, I've got you," he laughs.

"So did Dad come here often?" I ask, hoping the question sounds casual despite the fact that I'm shouting to make myself heard above the music.

"Not here so much, no. We only saw David in this neck of the wood once or twice. Mostly he was being wined and dined by the great and the good in Bordeaux. A tough assignment! But it was his work, after all, so maybe Catherine felt she didn't want to be in the way. A pity though. Liz would have enjoyed her company.

Yes, I think, unless she was too busy enjoying Dad's company instead.

I want to ask him more, but the music slows as the song comes to an end and Hugh makes a mock bow and kisses my hand. "Thank you my dear, that was most enjoyable and you are an excellent partner."

We pick our way back to the table where, I'm relieved to find, Celia has engaged Nigel in an animated conversation about the best local sources of click-lock flooring, a subject on which he apparently holds strong and expert opinions. I pour myself another glass of water and join the large lady I was sitting next to earlier – whose name I've already forgotten I'm afraid – and a group who are sharing their views on the best wines from local producers, on the basis of what seems to be some fairly extensive research. I'm interested to hear a couple of *domaines* mentioned that I haven't come across before, which are deemed to be particularly good value for money, and make a mental note to track them down at a later date. I'm looking for ideas for the dissertation I'm going to have to write in the second year of my Master of Wine course, (assuming I manage to pass the demanding practical and theory exams first), a daunting ten-thousand words on the subject of my choice. Maybe the 'other side' of Bordeaux will provide some inspiration. I resolve to visit in early autumn before the wine harvest begins.

Nigel materialises at my side, flushed with the excitement of yet another opportunity to demonstrate his extensive knowledge of the local DIY trade, or perhaps it's just the effect of one more glass of wine.

"There you are Gina," he slurs, interrupting the conversation and putting an overly-familiar arm round my shoulders. "That was quite a display you and old Hugh put on on the dance floor. Care to put me through my paces next?"

"That would have been lovely," I say, smiling politely whilst firmly removing his arm, "but the music seems to have stopped."

The Mayor has re-taken the microphone and is announcing that the firework display is about to begin, if everyone would like to make their way to the viewpoint.

Chattering and laughing, the crowd flows through the gap at the end of the square and re-groups where the hillside falls away steeply to the darkened valley floor below. I try to manoeuvre so that several other members of our party are between me and Nigel, but he's sticking to me like glue, (sticking being the operative word), persistently edging rather too far into my personal space. I catch sight of the Thibaults over to our right. Pierre has lifted Nathalie onto his shoulders so she can see and she's giggling and holding on tight to his dark curly head. Cédric, standing next to them, catches my eye and raises a hand in salute. Luc has joined a gang of young boys who are buzzing with excitement at the front of the crowd. They are repeatedly shooed back by the Mayor, although it's like trying to herd a swarm of flies.

The first rocket explodes above us and all faces turn to the starlit sky. The only sounds for the next quarter of an hour are the cracks of gunpowder and the oohs and aahs of delight. They've put on quite a show in this little town, and the same thing is happening all across France as, for one night at least, her people unite to celebrate the *liberté, egalité* and *fraternité* of their Republic.

When the display is over, the music starts up again in the square enticing the partygoers back to the disco. Some people begin to drift homewards and I head back to our table, intending to retrieve my basket and make my way back to the car parked in the Everetts' drive. But I'm intercepted by Nigel, who grabs my hand and pulls me onto the dance floor.

One of my favourite songs of the summer begins to play, I've heard it often on the radio, sung by a French artist called Grégoire. It's a pulsing tune that has everyone up on their feet. Its words are a poignant invitation to all who are alone to come and join the dance and they seem to be directed at people like Liz used to be, or like my mother is now, making their way on their own through life. Like me.

Or, indeed, like Nigel, who is now gyrating energetically in front of me. He appears to have no inhibitions on the dance floor, although sadly he also appears to have no sense of rhythm. All around us, couples have taken to the floor and all ages, shapes and sizes whirl by in formation. Little old ladies dressed in black dance past in decorous pairs. Hugh and Celia ceroc on by in perfect harmony. The Carla Bruni ballet dancer and her dishy husband whirl past elegantly. And the tall Lady Novelist waltzes by clutching Monsieur le Maire to her ample bosom. And in the middle of it all, Nigel and I hop clumsily, out of sync with the music and with each other. What he lacks in style he makes up for in enthusiasm though, and I duck to avoid his flailing arms, at the end of which his fingers are clicking in a way that may have been utterly groovy back in the 1960s but that is now simply cringe-worthy.

He moves in closer, obviously building up to some of his very best moves, and I step back to try to maintain a bit of distance between us. And in doing so tread heavily on the foot of the dancer behind me, who staggers and bumps into his own partner, almost sending her flying. And my mortification is complete as I realise the couple are Cédric and Marie-Louise. I shout an apology, but he has caught her and they whirl off, orbiting in their own accomplished jive, he with a smile and a shake of his head and she laughing as she spins away and back again into the steadying embrace of his outstretched arm.

The music finishes and, before it can segue into the next song, I thank Nigel and firmly turn and walk off the dance floor. He trots happily behind me, obviously pleased with his performance. We reach the table and he ensures my chagrin is complete with what is – as far as I'm concerned – his parting shot. "You know, Gina, you're really not at all a bad dancer."

*

Hugh, Celia and I walk back through the quiet streets of the village, the music and lights in the square fading behind us, and pick our way carefully the hundred yards or so along the darkened country road to the driveway of their house. They've left lights on which shine welcoming golden squares onto the gravel in front of the house.

"Come in and have a cup of coffee," the Everetts urge.

I hesitate. I wouldn't normally, but there is something I want to do, so I accept. While Celia bustles around boiling the kettle and clinking cups and saucers in the kitchen, Hugh opens the French doors and we settle ourselves on their terrace, the night air still warm, the noise of cicadas drowning out the distant sounds of the continuing revelry in the *place*.

Nonchalantly, as if it's a thought that's just occurred to me and not something I've mulled over endlessly through the dark hours of several recent sleepless nights, I say, "By the way Hugh, since I'm here I might as well take away Liz's urn. If it's not inconvenient for you of course."

"Why yes, not at all," he replies, glancing at me astutely. "We'll get it on your way out. Have you decided what you're going to do with it?"

Neither of us can quite bring ourselves to mention the word 'ashes'.

"Not yet, but I think she should be back in her own home until I do decide."

Celia appears with a tray of elegant china and the conversation turns to a review of the evening's festivities, (one of the best turn-outs ever, the committee will be pleased), and some final snippets of gossip about the other members of our party, (it turns out the husband of the large lady sitting next to me ran off with their cleaning lady a year ago – "they've moved to Gardonne and he's gone almost native! Poor Vanessa, so brave of her to stay on, though of course Franco-British week keeps her busy." Oh yes, so that was her name.)

As I take my leave, Hugh dives into his study and reappears with a cardboard box which he stows carefully on the floor of my car by the passenger seat. "Mind how you go Gina", he says in his gruff-yet-kind manner. I hug them both goodbye.

It's well after one a.m. when I get home, and Lafite runs out with an affronted squawk when I push open the door, indignant at having been incarcerated for the evening.

I set the cardboard box down on the kitchen table and open the flaps. Inside there's a neat black casket. I close the box up again, disguising the obscenity of death behind the plain brown packaging. It's too late to decide where to put it tonight. I'll think about it in the morning.

*

And so, of course, at four a.m. I'm wide awake and staring at the spare room ceiling. Lafite is curled up in a neat ball at the end of the bed, sleeping peacefully. But my mind is racing. That cup of coffee at the Everetts' was definitely a mistake.

Where am I going to scatter Liz's ashes and where am I going to store the casket until I get around to the act of scattering? Rationally, of course, it's just a pile of dust. Earth to earth and all that. But you can't get away from the fact that this dust is the last remnant of Liz's physical presence. And something that's been so dear and so familiar deserves – demands – to be treated with respect. No, respect is too cold a word. With love. Whatever she might have been to my father, she was a wonderful aunt - and friend – to me. One of the people on this planet who really loved me. And there aren't very many of those, I reflect with a sudden rush of self-pity.

Sorry, but four o'clock in the morning really is the loneliest of hours.

I pull myself together. OK, forget about where to scatter her ashes for the moment. Let's just decide where to put the damn urn in the meantime.

I don't think I can bring myself to put it on the mantelpiece in the kitchen. It would put me off my food to sit looking at a jar of mortal remains every mealtime. I could keep it in the study, but I'll be spending quite a bit of time in there when I really get started on my MW coursework and I don't want it to be a constant distraction. I could stick it in the broom cupboard in the utility room and try to forget about it, but that seems far too callous, so it'd be on my conscience. Which would mean I couldn't forget about it at all.

The sitting room seems like the best compromise. It's not a room Liz ever really used, but it seems respectful, with the air of formality that death demands, and at the same time is slightly out of the way of my daily life.

I know I'm not going to be able to get to sleep until I've moved the urn, so I slide out of bed carefully so as not to disturb Lafite and pad through to the kitchen. The house is so quiet all I can hear is the soft heartbeat tick of the clock above the fireplace. I fill the kettle and switch it on, pretending that a cup of camomile tea is just the soothing antidote I need to get back to sleep, but really to ruffle the surface of the silence with a little comfortingly domestic noise.

Gingerly, I remove the urn from the box and carry it through to the sitting room, tucking it into the crook of one arm as I turn the door handle and push the door open with a dry creak of its hinges. I put the casket of ashes on the coffee table between the two sofas which face each other conversationally. I pause for a moment and consider putting Dad's photo on the table beside the urn. But no, that would be too public an admission of what has gone before, even with the picture of the magpies covering the guilty secret as in the past. And it would also be too shrine-like. I can see Liz's wry smile mocking the idea. I pull the creaking door shut behind me, but then hesitate and open it again, pushing it ajar. It feels more companionable this way. And yes, I do realise how silly this is and that I'm making a huge issue out of what merely amounts to a jar full of dust. But since there's nothing I can do to bring Liz back, our last threads of connection - no matter how tenuous they may be – have become vitally important.

I pad back to bed, ignoring the now-quiet kettle with its wisp of silent steam and shivering a little despite the warmth of the July night. I slip back under the covers, pulling up the light quilt. Lafite, disturbed by the movement, wakes and stretches, then jumps down and stalks soundlessly out of the room, no doubt off on some nocturnal hunting expedition as I hear the clatter of the cat flap moments later.

Shame. I'd have liked his company in the dark hours that stretch between me and the dawn.

Chapter 9.

Hurrah, that's the last shutter finished. I've left the heavy ones that flank the doorway until the end and now they are neatly sanded, undercoated and painted and are resting on the trestles to dry. I'll ask the Thibault brothers to put them back on for me tomorrow. All the windows are now framed with the sage green panels and I pause for a moment on my way back to the house to survey my handiwork. Most satisfying.

I'm cleaning both the brushes and my green-spotted hands with white spirit at the kitchen sink, when there's a tap at door and a faint *"Coucou!"* I turn, and am delighted to find Mireille on the doorstep.

"I've come to inspect all the work that's been going on here, both yours and my sons'," she grins, her eyes bright as a bird's in the leather-brown folds of her face.

"Well you're just in time for tea too," I reply.

"Good, I hoped that might be the case."

We go out onto the terrace where Pierre is passing roof tiles up to Cédric. Raphael and Florian are elsewhere this week, finishing up other jobs before their break.

"The building inspector is here," I call, and the men pause in their work.

Peering down from his scaffolding perch, Cédric says in mock alarm, "Oh *mon dieu*, not that one! She's particularly difficult." He climbs down to join us.

They explain to their diminutive mother what they've been doing and she squints up at the newly rebuilt chimney and the surrounding roof with a critical gaze, before finally giving their work a nod of approval. "We're still waiting for the cowl for the chimney. It's on order at Lacombe and will only be in at the end of the month, but as it's summer Gina won't be lighting any fires I think," says Cédric. "And there's still the internal plastering to be done. But we'll come back after the holiday to finish that off."

"Are you going to use wet plaster or plasterboard?" she asks knowledgeably. (I have no idea what the difference is.)

"Plasterboard as it's easier and quicker. We can fix it between the beams and you won't be able to see the difference once it's painted," Cédric replies.

"Well," says Mireille somewhat doubtfully, "if Gina is happy with that solution..."

"I'm happy with whatever you recommend," I say to Cédric, mindful of the fact that they seem to be doing this part of the work as a favour and it would cost me considerably more to get a proper plasterer in. "Plasterboard sounds fine. After all, it's a simple farmhouse, not the palace at Versailles. And I'm really so grateful to your sons for all the work they've done," I continue, turning back to Mireille. "I know it's taken them away from other jobs. Now, let me go and get the tea things."

I carry the tray out and Mireille and I sit at the table while the brothers perch on the terrace wall. "We won't stop for long, we need to carry on to be sure of getting the tiles finished by Friday," they say.

I've made Pierre his usual tiny cup of strong black coffee, which he downs in one gulp, breaking off for a second from sending a couple of texts to do so. Mireille raises her eyebrows in surprise as Cédric accepts a cup of tea, and then shoots him a sharp glance. "Aha, I see you've managed to civilise one of my sons at least Gina."

Cédric grins and takes a couple of sips, but then stands up and nudges Pierre. "Come on Casanova, back to work."

Mireille and I enjoy a more leisurely chat and the conversation turns to last night's revelries.

"So did you enjoy our Bastille Day celebrations my dear?"

"Very much indeed. You rarely get a community coming together like that in England. At least the part I come from. It was fun. And you made all us foreigners feel very welcome."

"Ah, *oui*, the second occupation we call it. The first dates back to Eleanor of Aquitaine when this whole region belonged to the English kings. The second has happened a little more stealthily and a lot more recently. But we like having the English here. Everyone knows they make an important economic contribution to the region, especially when times aren't easy. And now with *la crise* in the wine industry it's even more important. Bordeaux isn't yet as badly hit as some other parts of France, but it's difficult all the same."

"I know it's getting harder to sell French wine in Britain," I say, "but surely the winemakers of Bordeaux can easily sell their production in France?"

"Not so much these days," Mireille shakes her head.

Pierre, pausing in the act of handing up another stack of tiles to Cédric, chips in, "It's not cool for the younger generation to drink wine these days. Whisky and beer are much more in."

And Cédric adds from on high, "Yes, and the French government isn't very supportive of the wine industry. In fact there's a big campaign against alcohol in general, because people are worried about the effects of drinking too much. But they're going to the opposite extreme, so the traditional French way of having a glass or two of wine with meals is dying out."

"But that's incredible," I say, astonished. "Wine is one of France's greatest commodities. It's a globally renowned brand. And you're telling me the government doesn't recognise how important this is to the country's economy? New World countries are far more geared up – they have huge marketing budgets to promote their wine industries and that's helped them to develop their markets around the world. If they're not able to compete with that, it's no wonder the French have lost so much ground. But it'll be a tragedy if the industry declines here. Just imagine the unemployment in this region, for a start! And there'll be even less individuality and character. We'll be left with just a few boring big brands that all taste the same. Like Australia, where most of the wines are made in big co-ops. Or the American super-brands that are on the shelves of every supermarket and corner-shop."

Mireille smiles. "We need more enlightened, intelligent people like you in the world, Gina," she jokes. "And the other English who have chosen to live here and support our winemakers of course." She pauses and shakes her head reflectively.

Then she looks at me appraisingly. "But you should write about it. You know about wine. You could help spread the word, tell people what's really happening in France. Wasn't your father a wine-writer?"

(She must know that from Liz, of course. What else did Liz tell her about Dad, I wonder. But that's not the point here. Focus.)

"Well, it's certainly important," I reply. "I don't think people have any idea that French wine is under so much threat."

"Yes," says Pierre, stacking roof tiles, "my friends are more bothered about saving whales and rainforests than the heritage and livelihood of their own region." He shrugs. "But maybe there's just no place for these traditions in the modern world. Most of the young feel it's too much hard work for too little return in wine these days. Unless you're in one of the top Médoc chateaus of course."

"Yes, but those are just the very tip of the pyramid," I say. "Those wines are something else altogether. Price-wise they're way out of reach of most people. We're talking about the majority of producers, who make interesting, good-quality wines with character, that sell for under twenty Euros a bottle. Actually, under ten in most cases. They're the ones that can offer individuality and variety to the industry as a whole. It would be vastly the poorer if they didn't exist."

"But do you know how hard it is for those winemakers to sell their wine?" asks Pierre. "On a small *domaine* they have to do everything - grow the grapes, make the wine and then do the marketing themselves too. They do try. They go to exhibitions, which cost a fortune, and they write letters and send out glossy brochures, but it's so difficult to get your wine tasted."

I think back, a little guiltily, to the piles of flyers, ranging from glossy to home-grown, that used to arrive on my desk at Wainright's, most of which I would put in the bin with scarcely a glance. But it would have been impossible to read them all, let alone taste every wine...

"You know Cédric," Mireille calls up to the roof where only her son's boots are visible as he lies on a ladder across the newly-mended area to fix more tiles in place, working methodically up towards the apex of the roof, "you should take Gina to visit the Cortinis. They can tell her more about the situation and show her their vineyard. It's one of the best around here," she adds, turning back to me. "Château de la Chapelle, just over in the next valley near St André."

I recognise the name as it's one of the *domaines* the ex-pat experts mentioned last night.

"That'd be interesting," I reply. "I've heard of the château and I'd very much like to taste their wines."

Cédric peers down from the roof. "I'll get in touch with Robert Cortini when we get back from Arcachon," he says. "In fact, we'll probably see him while we're at the *bassin*. He's usually there at this time too.

"Robert and Thomas are the sons of the château owner, Patrick Cortini," explains Mireille. "Patrick's getting on a bit now, but he still keeps an eye on the *chai*. Robert looks after the vines and Thomas does sales, but all three of them make the wine together."

"I'll look forward to meeting them in August," I say. I tell Mireille about the Master of Wine course. "I need to know a lot more about the technicalities of winemaking," I finish.

She nods approvingly. "It sounds like a tough course. But there's not much the Cortinis don't know about wine. They've been in the business for five generations. They'll be pleased to help you, I'm sure. And they're always delighted to meet anyone who's passionate about wine."

*

On Friday afternoon, the Thibaults' white lorry pulls into the courtyard. All four brothers have come to dismantle the scaffolding. Raphael inspects his younger siblings' work with a critical eye, and finally pronounces it to be *"pas mal."* It looks a lot better than *pas mal* to me. They've put a layer of new tiles underneath and then painstakingly cleaned the old tiles that were undamaged in the storm, slotting these back in place over the new ones to make a perfectly sung, watertight covering that is still weathered in subtle shades of terracotta and cream, so that the restored area blends with the rest of the roof. They've also cleaned off the moss from the remaining sections and replaced several cracked tiles, (and I'm sure that wasn't on the original remit). They sweep up the debris that's accumulated under the scaffolding and collect up the sheets of plastic and pallets that the new tiles were encased in, leaving everything neat and tidy.

"Can I offer you a drink to celebrate the end of the job and the start of your holidays?" I say.

"Non merci," replies Raphael. "We must get the lorry back to the yard and unload everything."

"And then go home to pack," adds Cédric. "Although Nathalie has had her bag packed for two days already. But Luc will take a little more organising, I suspect."

I suddenly realise how much I'm going to miss having them around.

And yes, of course, I do mean one of them in particular.

We shake hands as they leave. Cédric hangs back until last, and there's an awkward moment where I extend my hand and simultaneously he leans in to kiss my cheek. Politely ignoring the fact that I'm blushing bright red, he says, "*Au revoir* Gina. I haven't forgotten about your visit to Château de la Chapelle. I'll be in touch when I get back and have had a chance to organise things with the Cortinis."

"Thank you. I'm looking forward to it very much."

"And I'm looking forward to seeing you again very much, too," he replies, the deep-etched lines around his dark eyes crinkling in a smile.

Which wasn't what I said at all actually, I realise, when I replay the scene in my head afterwards, over and over again.

Chapter 10.

It's hot. Each day starts with a tantalising hint of coolness in the air - although there's not a wisp of cloud in the sky - which soon evaporates. The geraniums blaze brightly in their pots in the courtyard and on the terrace wall, reinvigorated by the long drink of water I've given them the evening before and a few hours' respite from the baking sun. But even at this time of day the background hum of cicadas underlies the fluting descant of morning birdsong, before the insects build to a frantic scream which drowns out every other sound and thought.

The heat becomes unbearable by midday, and in the garden leaves wilt and curl, their vitality drained. The grass is bleached to straw. Only the surrounding vines remain as abundantly and exuberantly green as ever, their strong roots able to penetrate to the very heart of the underlying limestone which holds water like a giant sponge. Perfectly formed bunches of grapes are starting to ripen beneath the neatly trimmed canopy of leaves. Overhead a buzzard floats languidly in the white hot sky, its nonchalantly lazy air not fooling the tiny furry creatures that huddle terrified in the grass below as its shadow passes.

Beaten into submission by the unremitting glare of the sun, I move indoors into the twilight of the house where I've closed all my newly-painted shutters in an attempt to keep the air here a little cooler.

It's too hot to eat much, but I make salads of the big misshapen tomatoes that I buy in the market each week, the concentrated tang of their red flesh dazzling my taste-buds just as the sunlight does my eyes. I scatter torn leaves of peppery dark green basil over them and sop up their juices with chunks of crusty bread. Three flavours are all you need to make a meal here.

After lunch I have a siesta, something I've never done before in my life. But in this heat it's almost impossible to move, until about four o'clock when the sun's rays begin to lengthen and soften just a little. So I lie on one of the battered plastic loungers in the shade or, when it's too stiflingly hot to be outdoors at all, on the bed in the spare room where it's cooler and there's an intact ceiling. Sometimes I read, but more often I just lie on top of the covers, plugged into my iPod. And usually I sink into a deep, dreamless, heat-drugged sleep. I know it won't help the night-time insomnia, but at least it's one way of catching up on my sleep deficit. At first I feel guilty about indulging in a midday nap, but I soon realise there's nothing to feel guilty for – it's not as if there's anybody around to judge me, nor anything else I should be doing.

I've ordered some of the books I need for the Master of Wine course, so occasionally the bright yellow van of *La Poste* appears up the drive to deliver another brown parcel. It's a daunting reading list.

I'm fairly confident about the tasting side of the course since I've had years of expert tuition by my father and Harry Wainright. There'll be practical exams to assess my "organoleptic competencies" and knowledge of world wines, but I had a lot of opportunity to taste wines from far and wide in my buying career, so it's just going to be a question of keeping up-to-date and making sure I've covered some of the less common regions and wines. I know Harry will help me with this – he's remained in touch and offered support. And I can always ask Annie for help when it comes to the New World. (She's now working for WineLand, the company that bought out Wainright's, although she wasn't thrilled at the resulting move to their Head Office in Croydon). So once the course is underway I'll plan a trip back to England for a few tasting sessions.

The other sections of the syllabus look as if they're going to be a lot more taxing. There's a whole section on the production of wine which includes such topics as the chemical composition of grapes, pests and diseases and the intricacies of fermentation. I managed to scrape a pass for GCSE Chemistry but that was years ago and I can't say anything at all has stuck. There'll be two three-hour exam papers on this section. And then I need to know about "The Business of Wine" which includes a section on financial and commercial awareness, so my finely-tuned understanding of accounting and economics (ha!) will be brought into play here. And finally there's a topic entitled "Trends and Challenges facing wine producing countries and regions". And as I'm rapidly discovering, there's enough material in Bordeaux alone to fill the whole of the three-hour exam paper on this one, let alone what's going on in the rest of the wine-producing world.

Every time I look through my well-thumbed copy of the syllabus, I feel completely overwhelmed. How could I ever have imagined I'd be up to this course? There are two hundred and fifty Masters of Wine in the world. I used to think this was a lot. But now I realise it's a tiny number. It feels as if I'm trying to join a very exclusive club, and I'm very much afraid they're not going to want me for a member. Through my doubts I can hear Liz saying, "Go on Gina, give it a go! Who knows where it might take you." And Dad saying, "You can do it. You're as good as anyone else. Anything that's worth doing is a challenge."

I feel like retorting, "Go away. I'm not talking to either of you right now." But the most annoying thing about people who are dead is that you can't answer them back.

Supposing I do actually manage to pass all four exams and the practical tests too, I then have to produce my ten thousand word dissertation. And in this heat I can hardly summon the energy to press the 'select' button on my iPod. But it's going to be a long winter I suspect, and maybe by then I'll even be glad to have so much work to keep me busy.

One afternoon I'm rudely awoken from my midday nap by the ringing of the phone. I've been so deeply asleep that it takes a second or two to register that it's Annie calling.

"Hi hon, how are you? My god, were you asleep? Sorry to wake you up. But how decadent at this time of day! While some of us are slaving away here in the pulsating centre-of-the-universe that is Croydon. I'm just ringing to see what your plans are in the next few weeks. Are you completely snowed under with visitors?"

I contemplate the lonely days and nights stretching ahead and reply that I have precisely nothing in the diary.

"Oh good, well can I come and stay? I thought I'd pop over. I'm dying to come and see where you are and have a proper catch-up."

I'm wide awake immediately, delighted at the prospect. "Come whenever. Stay as long as you can. Oh Annie, I can't wait to see you!"

"Good. I'll book flights. Bergerac's the best to fly into isn't it? I'll email you my dates. Things are pretty quiet here at work so I can probably get away next week or the week after. Are either of those ok? Great. See you soon then. Big hugs."

Hooray. Company at last. And it's my age. And it speaks English. And it's my best friend.

*

I stand outside the customs shed at Bergerac airport at the back of a small crowd of people waiting to meet friends and loved ones off the Stansted flight. Most of the crowd are English and several have brought along their dogs who are busy trying to sniff one another's bottoms, winding their leads around the legs of anyone who gets in the way. The odd volley of barking breaks out when the sniffee takes exception to the overly-enthusiastic attentions of the sniffer. Strange, this habit of bringing animals to the airport, lending it the charmingly whimsical air of a village dog-show. I've only ever seen it here at Bergerac, so maybe it's a particularly British ex-pat thing.

I peer into the gloom of the arrivals hall, from which people are now beginning to emerge, trying too hard not to look self-conscious as they are met by a sea of expectant faces and breaking into relieved smiles when they find the one they're searching for. I'm looking for a sultry brunette, this being the last guise in which I saw Annie, so am caught off-guard when a curvaceous platinum blonde steps through the door and begins waving at me enthusiastically. I should have known. She was sure to get back in touch with her inner blonde before too long.

I've been feeling a bit of trepidation about Annie's visit. Whilst we're very good friends, it has dawned on me that we've never actually spent such an extended period of time together, sleeping under the same roof. There was that time we went to Vinexpo of course, back in the boom years when Wainright's was a thriving business and Harry was feeling particularly flush. We stayed in a B&B in Bordeaux for three nights, spending the days tramping through the halls of the vast exhibition centre which hosts this world wine event every other year, and the evenings at restaurants along the *quais* in the city centre. But that doesn't really count. It's not the same as having someone staying with you in your own home.

However, the minute I see Annie tottering towards me in a pair of perilously high strappy sandals, an oversized pair of sunglasses pushed back on top of her bright crown of hair, wheeling her large suitcase behind her and grinning from ear to ear, I know it's going to be fine. We hug, already simultaneously talking and laughing, and I help her drag her case to the car.

She loves the house, exclaiming enthusiastically at the setting, the space and her pretty room. I've moved back upstairs to let her have the spare room. The ceiling above my bed is still a rough cross-hatch of wooden laths supporting the roof tiles and a neat new silver lining of insulating material. It gives the room an industrial air, but at least it's weather-tight, if a little stuffy in this heat. I've taken to keeping my makeup in the fridge after my mascara melted into a sticky black mess and leaked all over the dressing-table.

Once she's unpacked, we sit on the terrace in the balmy evening air and Lafite, curious at the arrival of this newcomer, jumps into her lap and begins purring loudly as she strokes his furry head. I open a cold bottle of Clairet, which Annie pronounces "yummy", (a technical term us highly trained wine tasters like to use), and leans back in her chair, stretching luxuriantly.

"God, look at my awful pasty arms compared to yours," she says. "I've definitely got some serious work to do to lose this Croydon pallor in the next week. You look wonderful Gina, if a bit on the skinny side. Your new life in France obviously agrees with you."

"Well it's not as if I've got a lot on my plate at the moment. No job, no man, it's the secret of stress-free life. Or rather no life at all. So I've been able to put in a good deal of sunbathing time of late."

"Yes, but I'm full of admiration for you making a start on the MW course. It's something I'm always meaning to get round to but there's never the time. It's bloody difficult too – not sure I could handle it at all."

"But then you've got a very full-time job. How is business these days?" I ask.

"Pretty dire actually, between you and me, but I'm lucky to be in work at all so I shouldn't complain. The commute to Croydon is hellish. Sales are way down across the board, although compared to everyone else on the high street WineLand seems to be surviving ok. Our philosophy of pile 'em high and sell 'em low is the right one in a recession. Especially if you want to stand a chance against the supermarkets. And of course New World wines are in right now, and thanks to their currencies they tend to be good value, so I'm in the right place even if times are hard."

"I know," I sigh. "I was in the wrong area really on the French side. Completely out of fashion."

"Well, give it long enough and it'll come back in again, "says Annie philosophically. "It's like anything trendy – if you're selling classic cut trousers and flares are in, you either have to wait until straight-cut comes back or start selling flares yourself. One day the recession will be over and people will see the light and come back to French wines."

"Aha!" I laugh, "so are you finally admitting that France makes better wines than the New World?"

This debate has been the subject of long-running banter between the two of us for years.

"Not at all," replies Annie haughtily. "But it's a question of style. Plus the fact that generally people are lazy and will pick up the first vaguely recognisable bottle that comes to hand in the supermarket."

"You're right," I say with a sigh. "It's the culture of instant gratification that rules in Britain these days. But as we both know, not all French wines are expensive and inaccessible. Some producers have even started making New World-style wines, which is ironic. It used to be that the rest of the world mimicked France, but the wheel has turned and now France is having to mimic the rest of the world."

"Yes, but of course in that endearingly stubborn way of theirs most French producers would rather go bust than be untrue to their heritage," retorts Annie. "Just look at the strict rules of the *Appellation Controlée* system. No other country has to comply with such rigorous controls. I do admire the cussedness of the French, I'll give you that. They certainly don't believe in making life easy for themselves and you have to give them credit for caring so passionately about their winemaking. It's just that the New World is good at manufacturing wines that suit what people are looking for – cheap and cheerful, uncomplicated, accessible. A bit like what a man looks for in a woman really, now I come to think of it. Speaking of which, what's the local talent like here? Any sexy French gentlemen callers?"

"Well unless your taste runs to oily estate agents who've seen the back of fifty then not really. Although I have been hotly pursued by an English guy of late."

"Well that sounds promising," Annie replies, delighted at the prospect of some hot gossip. "Tell me more!"

"Yup, his name's Nigel and he has a comb-over. Oh and he's desperate to share the inner workings of his septic tank with me. That really is about as good as it gets around here. I'm afraid you've come to the wrong place if you're in search of a week of rampant holiday sex. There's been a definite drought of late, and I'm not just talking about the weather."

"Well it's high time you came back to Britain and your Auntie Annie will have to see if she can't come up with someone. I'm sure I can find a suitable candidate in my little black book."

"No thank you," I say firmly. "I don't fancy the idea of anyone you've already chewed up and spat out. And anyway, I'm still off men after the whole Roddy saga. How does that old joke go? What's the difference between a man and a catfish?"

"I don't know, what is the difference between a man and a catfish?" Annie dutifully replies.

"One's a scum-sucking bottom-feeder. And the other one's a kind of fish."

She cackles appreciatively, then frowns. "Rubbish! Never mind fish. It's just like riding a horse. You have to get straight back in the saddle. Or so I understand. Not that I've ever ridden a horse..." and our conversation descends into the sort of raucously hilarious girl-chat I've so been missing.

At the end of the evening, light-headed and light-hearted from a potent combination of friendship, wine and laughter, we finally say goodnight and Annie, weaving slightly, disappears off to the guest room clutching a large bottle of Evian. As I shut the back door for the night, I realise the cicadas have finally gone quiet, perhaps giving up in the face of such shrill competition from the terrace. In the velvety darkness the faint hoot of an owl drifts across the newly-fallen silence.

*

Next morning, putting the kettle on to boil for a much-needed cup of coffee to get the day started, I discover we're out of milk. *Merde*. Never mind, some croissants would be nice too, so I jump in the car and nip down to Super U before there's any sign of life from Annie.

I get back to find her clattering mugs in the kitchen. She's wearing shorts and flip-flops, the straps of a bikini showing under her camisole top.

"I've fed Lafite," she says, gesturing to where he's crunching the last few morsels in his bowl. "Such a honey, he spent the night curled up on my bed."

"Huh, what a tart that cat is," I retort.

"Oh and someone phoned," she continues. "A French bloke. Trouble is, he was talking so fast I couldn't make out half of what he said. Something about *une heure*. So I think he's going to call back in an hour's time. Or maybe at one o'clock, Anyway, he'll definitely call back."

"OK. Probably the stonemasons," I reply, hoping I sound nonchalant. "They're due back from holiday about now so they're probably phoning to arrange when they're coming to finish fixing the upstairs ceiling." I don't want to admit to myself how much I'm looking forward to seeing Cédric again. And there's absolutely no way I'd admit it to Annie.

I busy myself pouring the milk into a jug and putting breakfast things on a tray. "Shall we have this outside?"

"Lovely, I'm planning on spending every possible second in the sun today. Have to get some serious tanning in."

"Well, I hope you've brought the Factor 30. You'll be needing it by midday, or you'll end up with a truly British dose of sunburn," I laugh.

After breakfast we spread ourselves out on the sun-loungers. Annie's brought copies of all the latest English magazines with her so we settle down in our bikinis, with Aretha on the iPod and Vogue, Harper's and Hello scattered around us.

After a while, she puts down her magazine to re-baste her skin with suntan lotion and turn onto her front. "Back to what we were saying last night about French wines," she says. "Are you seriously telling me local producers in Bordeaux, the sacred heartland of the industry in France, are making New World-style wines these days?"

"Yup," I reply. "In fact I've got some that I bought from a château near here the other day. They've given it an English name, simplified the labels, even put the grape-type on the front. The wines are interesting – up-front fruit, ready for drinking young, but I reckon they've still kept in a twist of French subtlety too. You can taste them if you're interested."

"Love to. You know me, I never rest in the diligent pursuit of something new for the discerning clients of WineLand."

Which reminds me, I haven't yet shared with Annie my theory about good wines being like good sex, engaging the mind as well as the senses. So I proceed to enlighten her and she gleefully agrees.

"Yes, you're so right. And bad wine, like bad sex, should be sniffed out in the preliminary stages and avoided altogether!" she hoots. "OK, let's put your theory to the test then. Bring on the wines."

I shove my feet into my flip-flops – the terrace paving is now scalding hot – and go indoors to retrieve a selection of wines from my embryonic collection. To make things a little more challenging, I add a couple of bottles of Californian wine from the selection I brought over with me, and I nip upstairs to find a scarf to use as a blindfold. As an afterthought, I grab the phone from the study and put it on the kitchen table so we can hear it from the terrace. Just in case the caller from earlier rings back. And especially in case it's Cédric, although I'm trying to ignore this thought.

"Right," I say, reappearing outside and putting the cardboard box of bottles on the table, in the shade of the large sun umbrella that covers it. "You're tasting blind, and I'm going to make sure there's no cheating." I tie the silk scarf over Annie's eyes. "Are you going to be spitting or swallowing this morning?"

"Don't even get me started!" screeches Annie at this well-worn joke. "Though given the early hour and the heat, I think it would be wise to spit on this occasion. Not like me, I know darling."

I nip back into the kitchen to collect a jug to use for a spittoon and then I open the first bottle. She sniffs the wine carefully, considering, and then tastes it, slurping it noisily around her mouth to aerate the wine and draw out its flavour.

"Interesting. An oaked white. A bit on the heavy side. I'm getting pear and a strong taste of vanilla. Not quite dry, there's a sweetish aftertaste. But hang on. Is it a Chardonnay? In which case it's not one of your local wines, unless it really is something very ground-breaking and they've decided to go the *vin de pays* route. Are you trying to trick me, Peplow?" she says, suspicion dawning. "I reckon this really is a New World wine. I'm guessing it's either Australian or American? In fact I'm going to say American given the sweetness and the strong vanilla in the oak. Not bad, but not really lighting my candle."

"Most impressive Ms McKenzie. Just checking your taste-buds haven't atrophied in my absence. It's that Napa Valley Chardonnay that we used to sell at

Wainright's. Originally selected by you I believe. OK, next wine."

I ease the cork out of a bottle of the local white.

"Hmm, interesting," muses Annie, sniffing her glass repeatedly. "Now this is something entirely different. Crisp, dry, but with good fruit and an almost floral scent too. A hint of oak maybe?"

She sips, slurps, spits.

"Wow. So complex. Difficult to tell the varietals. Definitely some Sauvignon. And, because I think this is one of your local numbers I'm going to say Sémillon too. But that floral twist is amazing – I can't quite pin it down – and the oak is really subtle. God this is good. In fact, so good I may even have to have a swallow..."

She sips again, swirling the wine around her mouth to draw out every nuance of the flavour. "OK Peplow, your theory works. This is definitely the equivalent of good sex." And then, in irrepressible Annie McKenzie style, she throws back her blindfolded head and commences an impression of noisy gratification that makes Meg Ryan's famous scene in the film 'When Harry Met Sally' look like Mary Poppins. Her cries of "Yes, yes, oh god, yes" mingle with Aretha's raucous vocals from the iPod where, backed up by The Eurythmics, she's declaring that "sisters are doing it for themselves," and I double up with laughter at the appropriateness of the musical accompaniment to Annie's act.

And then, to my absolute horror, I glimpse a movement from the corner of my eye and realise that we're not alone. Wheeling round, I find Cédric and Pierre who have just rounded the corner of the house carrying a long ladder between them and are now standing dumbstruck, surveying the scene in front of them. And, oh dear, I have to admit it doesn't look good.

I grab my cotton shirt from the back of the sun-lounger and hastily pull it on. Annie, blissfully unaware in her blindfolded state, carries on hamming up her appreciation of the wine, her ample curves generously filling her somewhat skimpy bikini.

Pierre is now grinning from ear to ear, while Cédric, who's carrying a large cement cube as well as his end of the ladder, looks somewhat bemused at this apparition.

Annie comes to the end of her grand command performance as the song fades out and, suddenly aware of the awkward silence that has fallen, she pulls the scarf off her eyes.

"Oops!" she says cheerfully, not at all abashed at the sight of the two brothers, "didn't realise we had company." And she bounces across the terrace – bounce being the operative word – to shake hands.

"*Bonjour* Gina," says Cédric turning to me and taking my awkwardly proffered hand too. "I'm so sorry, we didn't mean to disturb you. We did knock at the kitchen door but I don't think you could hear us."

No, well, I suppose we were making a bit of a racket. One of us in particular anyway.

"I phoned earlier," he continues, "to let you know we'd be coming round in an hour's time. The cowl for the chimney has arrived." He nods at the cement block which he's put down on the ground beside the ladder.

"Ah," I say nodding in what I hope is a dignified, calm cool and collected manner in spite of my state of undress and the fact that I'm in the company of a similarly scantily clad female, surrounded by discarded clothes, magazines and enough bottles of wine for quite a respectable party at ten o'clock on a weekday morning. "So that was the message. It lost a little in translation I'm afraid."

Oh god, I think, he's looking incredibly handsome after his holiday – tanned and more relaxed than usual. And then, to my confusion, I realise he hasn't relinquished my hand and I'm in no hurry to relinquish his either. A realisation that immediately makes me drop it, as if it's burning as hotly as the flagstones of the terrace or my own flaming cheeks.

"How was your holiday?" I ask.

"Great thanks. We had a good time. Nathalie and Luc loved being at the beach with all their cousins so it was very easy. And Marie-Louise's father has a boat at the *bassin* so we had some good outings in it. Do you sail?"

"Yes, I love it," I reply. "Though I haven't been for years. I used to go with my father when I was young."

"Well you'll have to come along sometime," he smiles.

Great, I think, pulling at the hem of my shirt and wishing it covered more of the flesh of my legs. That'll be a fun outing, sitting in your wife's father's boat and lusting after her husband. But I smile and nod with what I hope looks like enthusiasm.

"You seem to be a little – er – occupied... Would you like us to come back another time?" asks Cédric. "It'll only take a few minutes to fix this on top of the chimney."

Annie's grasp of French is pretty slender, but she clearly gets the gist of this last bit. "Oh, don't mind us," she says cheerfully. "Please carry on."

"Yes, do go ahead," I say. "I'll just clear a bit of space for the ladder." I scoop up an armful of clothes and magazines and scurry inside where, thankfully, I pull on my denim skirt and smooth down my hair, trying to regain a little composure.

I come back out into the bright sunshine. Pierre is holding the ladder while Cédric climbs up, carefully balancing the heavy cowl as he goes. Annie, not the least abashed, is perching on the terrace wall, rather coquettishly it has to be said, looking on appreciatively.

When Cédric descends a few minutes later, Annie gestures to the bottles of wine on the table. "Would you like a drink?" she asks. "We were just tasting some very good local wines."

The two brothers clearly find the invitation hilarious. "It's good that you enjoy them so much," says Cédric trying to keep a straight face, "but *non merci*, we have to get to another job. There's a lot to do as we're just back."

"Please excuse us," adds Pierre still grinning broadly at Annie, "but Raphael is a slave driver and he'll already be wondering where we are. Another time perhaps..."

As they pick up the ladder ready to leave, Cédric turns to me. "We'll be back in about two weeks' time to finish the work on the ceiling upstairs. I'm afraid we're a bit busy catching up with work after the holidays at the moment, so it can't be any sooner. I'll phone you to give you better warning next time though," he says with a roguish glint in his eye. "Oh, and one other thing. I saw the Cortinis at the *bassin*. They'd be delighted to show you round at Château de la Chapelle and let you taste their wines. They suggested we visit on Friday evening, but perhaps you'd rather wait until your friend has departed? Although she'd be very welcome to join us if it would be of interest."

"That's so kind. I'm sure you'd love to come along, wouldn't you Annie? She's in the wine business so she might be a good contact for them."

"OK, great. I'll come and pick you up about 5.30 then."

They load the ladder onto the back of Cédric's pickup and disappear down the drive.

Back on the terrace, Annie is sitting at the table in the shade of the sun umbrella awaiting my return. "Well, well, well Miss Peplow," she crows gleefully. "You are a dark horse. Why didn't you tell me about the hunky French workmen?"

"I don't know what you mean," I retort haughtily. "They've just been doing the repair work here. Their mother is my neighbour. They've been very kind and helpful, that's all."

"Oh come off it!" she scoffs. "I haven't seen so much chemistry since my science teacher dropped a whole jar of sodium into a sinkful of water."

"Why," I ask, seizing the opportunity for a diversion, "what happens when you drop sodium into water?" Sometimes Annie surprises me with the things she knows.

"Let's just say the results are pretty explosive," she replies, "but don't go trying to change the subject. What's going on between you and that good-looking older brother?"

"Precisely nothing," I say firmly. "He happens to be happily married to a gorgeous French wife and has two lovely children to whom he is utterly devoted."

"Well he wasn't behaving like someone who's entirely happily married. He couldn't take his eyes off you. He definitely fancies you – there was about forty thousand volts of electricity between you when he was holding your hand. And don't tell me you don't fancy him back. I know you. Gina Peplow, and you're absolutely hopeless at lying so don't even bother trying."

"Ok, ok," I hold up my hands in defeat, plonking myself down on a chair beside her and reaching for the open bottle of Chardonnay. Sod it, it is about time for elevenses after all. "I do like him. And I get the feeling he likes me too. But there's no way I'm having an affair with a married man, especially one whose mother is my friend and neighbour. And his children are wonderful – you just couldn't hurt them. His wife's really nice too..." I trail off lamely.

"So if it's all so perfect, why does he look at you like a starving man who's just caught sight of a Big Mac and fries?"

"Please," I laugh, "at least credit me with being something a little more classy than the equivalent of a trip to Mcdonald's."

"Ok then, a starving man in a Michelin-starred restaurant. Whatever. The French are supposed to be far more cool about this sort of thing. Perhaps he's looking for a *ménage à trois*. A sort of Vicky Cristina Barcelona. Only set in Sainte Foy La Grande."

"Doesn't have quite the same ring to it somehow, does it? And I'm not the slightest bit interested in being part of anything like that if it is the case. Which, anyhow, I strongly doubt."

"Ah, the eternal triangle," says Annie sagely. And then, lightening up, she says "Now, enough about the men in your life. Or not in your life, as the case might be. Let's get back to the serious business of tasting these wines. Where we before we were so opportunely interrupted?"

I pull the cork from the next bottle and, speaking of triangles, think of Liz's lonely life, wondering for the umpteenth time what exactly her role was in my parents' relationship. Pulling myself together quickly, before Annie's uncanny powers of observation detect another secret that I'm keeping from her, I slosh some red into our glasses. "Right then, see what you think of this," I say. "Let's see if it has the same interesting effect as the white..."

Chapter 11.

Promptly at five-thirty on Friday evening, Cédric's dark blue pickup pulls into the courtyard. He jumps out and comes to knock at the door to the kitchen, where I've been hovering for the last half-hour trying to pretend I'm busily engaged in various domestic tasks. The sink and its taps, under the window which is – coincidentally – the best vantage point to look out at the courtyard, are gleaming I've cleaned them so thoroughly, and now I'm scrubbing my hands to try and get the smell of disinfectant off them again.

My heart gives a little lurch at the sight of him. He looks freshly scrubbed himself, in jeans and a neatly-ironed shirt, the sleeves rolled up to show a length of muscular, tanned forearm. Trying hard to suppress a surge of unruly hormones that suddenly makes me very conscious of every part of my own body, I open the door with a gracious and composed smile. For once I've had time to prepare and so at least I'm a bit more elegantly groomed than on many of Cédric's previous visits.

He kisses me hello, most decorously of course on either cheek, but nonetheless it occurs to me that it's the first time he's done so when we're alone. Oh god, how sad am I? It's just the French equivalent of shaking hands for heaven's sake, and I'm being completely pathetic.

"I'll just go and see if Annie's ready," I say brightly, my voice sounding, to my guilty ears at least, unnaturally high and nervous.

She's in her room putting the finishing touches to her makeup. "Is he here? Oh good." She looks at me appraisingly and reaches out to brush my cheek with her thumb. "An eyelash," she explains. "But other than that you'll do. You scrub up quite nicely you know. Now let's go get him!"

"Annie," I say firmly. "We're not getting anyone. And especially not him. He's out of bounds."

"Ok, ok, whatever you say, Little Miss Celibate. Just seems like a bit of a waste to me, that's all."

I glare at her sternly. She makes a zipping gesture across her lips. "Not another word, I promise," she says, still grinning broadly, obviously relishing the prospect of watching me squirm.

She clambers into the narrow back seat of the pickup, displaying a good deal of brown thigh and just a hint of bottom-cleavage for the benefit of Cédric who is politely holding the door open for her. Isn't there a golden rule about no miniskirts or butt-cracks over the age of thirty? If there's not, there should be. Although that still wouldn't stop Annie from flaunting it shamelessly.

Somewhat more decorously, I hope, I climb into the front passenger seat and Cédric closes the door and comes round to jump into the drivers' seat. I can't help noticing his capable hands on the steering wheel as he starts the truck and we pull away. Oh god, concentrate woman! I catch a glimpse of Annie's twinkling eyes which are looking at me from the rear-view mirror.

"So Cédric, tell us about the Cortinis. Have they owned Château de la Chapelle for long?" I ask airily, determined to maintain a business-like tone.

"Yes, for several generations. Patrick, who is the father of Robert and Thomas, owns the château now. His grandfather came from Italy to work there at the beginning of the last century and he ended up marrying the owner's daughter. Hence the Italian surname. So the property's been in the family one way or another for hundreds of years. Patrick's nearly seventy now, but he's still very involved in the winemaking and keeps a close eye on the boys. Robert, who was in my class at school, is in charge of the vines and Thomas, who's two years younger, does the marketing. Eventually Patrick will hand over to his sons, but he finds it hard to stop. His wife left him about twenty years ago and so the château and the wines have been his whole life ever since. Keeping busy stops him from getting lonely I suppose."

Annie, who's hanging over the back of my seat to listen to the conversation, asks me to translate this last bit. "Blimey," she says, "who'd she leave him for? Most women would love to be married to a château-owner. It doesn't get much more romantic than that!"

"Sadly winemaking's not a very romantic existence in reality," replies Cédric. "As you probably know, it's brutally hard work, long hours and low returns. Madame Cortini got fed up with it all in the end and, once the boys left school she went off with a dentist from Bordeaux who was a much better proposition. She's been far happier with her new life ever since. Not that the boys see that much of her nowadays."

So much for the fairytale life in a castle then. Modern day princesses take a far more pragmatic approach, it would seem.

"Robert's married and has three kids, the same age as Luc and Nathalie and then one a bit younger," Cédric continues. "Thomas is still a bachelor though – he spends a lot of time on the road trying to sell their wine."

I can almost see Annie's ears pricking up at this last bit of information and she raises her eyebrows at me in the mirror. I'm not sure whether she's interested on my behalf or her own but either way the prospect of an unattached male of around our age has got her attention.

Steadfastly ignoring this diversion, I firmly guide the conversation back to the safer ground of the wines they make and the production methods they use. Cédric, his attention fixed on the traffic which is quite busy at this time on a Friday evening, even on these little country roads, professes not to know that much about the technicalities. "But here we are," he says, swinging the pickup into the driveway of Château de la Chapelle, "so you can ask the experts."

It's a pretty *domaine*. The driveway, which runs up the slope of the hill, is flanked by an avenue of dark green cypresses and beyond them on either side the rows of vines run in precisely parallel lighter green lines, their tops neatly trimmed to a uniform height. Just visible beneath the leaves nestle the clusters of ripening grapes, their black skins softened to shades of velvety purple-grey by their fine coating of bloom.

We park in front of the house, an elegantly proportioned building. The hillside dips slightly behind it and then rises again, forming a natural bowl which is perfect for the cultivation of vines. On the skyline sits a little stone church with a tall, pointed steeple. "That's the chapel of Saint André from which the château takes its name," explains Cédric, pointing it out.

We walk round the side of the house to a yard where a large tractor, towing a fearsome-looking trimmer whose blades glint in the evening sun, is being effortlessly reversed under the roof of a lean-to shed for the night.

"There's Robert," says Cédric, raising a hand in salute. "Good timing, it looks like he's just finished for the day."

A stocky, compact man in a green boiler-suit climbs down from the cab and the two men greet each other with the hug and double kiss that still seems so foreign to us more cold-blooded Brits. Then Robert turns to greet us, wiping his hands on the cotton of his neat overalls before shaking ours.

"Come into the *chai*," he says. "My father and Thomas are inside I think."

In the gloom of the vast shed, the walls are lined with gleaming stainless steel vats. A pair of legs clad in an immaculately pressed pair of khaki trousers protrudes from the small door in the front of one of these and a muffled stream of expletives can be heard echoing off the walls inside it.

Cédric and Robert grin at one another and Robert turns to Annie and me. "Excuse me for one moment," he says, and walks across to tap the legs. There's a brief pause and then a renewed outburst of cursing, louder than before. "Papa," Robert perseveres, "we have company."

The legs back up out of the vat and Patrick Cortini emerges fully, a handsome elderly man with a shock of white hair and a thick white moustache. His face creases into delighted smiles at the sight of us and he comes over to shake hands.

"What charming young ladies," he beams, gallantly declaring himself *enchanté* to make our acquaintance. "Please forgive me," he says, "but some idiot hasn't cleaned out the *cuves* properly, so I'm having to do them again myself. We're getting everything ready for the harvest in a few weeks' time and as usual it's up to me to make sure everything's done right."

Robert continues to smile serenely, even though this dig is clearly aimed at him and his brother. He turns to us and says calmly, "Actually the *cuves* are perfectly clean, but Papa finds it impossible to admit that anyone else is capable of doing anything properly." He gives his father a fond hug. "Still, it keeps you out of trouble I suppose."

A slightly younger and taller version of Robert materialises from an office in one corner of the *chai* and Cédric introduces us to Thomas.

"So you are in the wine trade?" he asks in English, with a very charming French accent.

"Well, I used to be, but not now. Annie, however, is a buyer for one of the biggest chains in the UK," I explain.

"But Gina is an expert too. She is currently doing a course to get some higher qualifications," adds Cédric.

"In that case it is an even greater pleasure to welcome the two of you to Château de la Chapelle," Thomas smiles. "Shall we show you round the cellar first and then we can go and taste the wines?"

It's a well-run operation. Annie and I have visited enough wineries in our time to be able to spot signs of sloppiness or taking shortcuts and there are none here.

Patrick proudly shows us the nuts and bolts of the cellar, the gleaming, surgically clean steel vats; the vast yellow Vaslin press, the de-stemming machine and assorted pumps and long coils of plastic tubing, stowed in the corners for now but ready for action when the hectic days of harvesting begin next month. They show us the bottling room where the machinery stands quiet for the moment amidst orderly metal cages of filled bottles, waiting to be labelled and have the capsules put over their corks when orders come in. And they usher us through to the hallowed coolness of the barrel cellar where the previous year's wine rests quietly in softly scented barrels of French oak, taking on the wood's subtle flavours for a final twist of finesse and smoothness.

Our tour finally over, Thomas leads us to the back of the house where a shady terrace gives onto the vineyard. We sit down at a table spread with a checked cloth and Robert tells us about his work in the vines. "We practice *culture raisonnée*, using as few pesticides and chemicals as possible and encouraging the vines to find their own balance and strength. It's not quite organic, but it's reassuring to have the treatments to fall back on if necessary, for example if we have a cool, damp summer, like last year, when mildew can become a problem and threaten the harvest. Of course, under the French *appellation controlee* system we're not allowed to irrigate or use fertilisers like the New World producers do. The wine has to be a reflection of its *terroir*, the vines growing only where it's appropriate for them to do so given the conditions of soil and climate, that's the French philosophy. But you will know all this already of course," he smiles at us.

Thomas adds, "People in Britain tend to ignore the fact that French wine is often a more natural product than its non-European counterparts. And of course, wine from Europe has less far to travel than New World wines, so it's a far greener product with a much smaller carbon footprint. These things are becoming more important, I think, and we need to get the message across."

Annie agrees, but explains that her role at WineLand is very much on the New World side. "There's a place for wines from all over the world in the UK market though," she argues, loyal to her clientele. "The English are generally quite a sophisticated and well-informed bunch."

Patrick has disappeared into the house and emerges carrying a tray laden with glasses and bottles. Thomas leaps up to help his father, deftly opening the two reds to let them breathe a little before we begin with the whites. They're delicious – an unoaked Sauvignon Blanc with just a hint of Sémillon to soften and balance the acidity, and a more complex oaked wine, heavier on the Sémillon made in a more sophisticated, almost Burgundian style. Then there's a crisp Clairet, the perfect wine for a hot summer's evening with its mouth-watering cherry flavours. And finally we taste the two reds, again one oaked and one not. They're really well made Clarets, smooth, fruity Merlot with a tantalising edge of spicy Cabernet Sauvignon.

Annie seems to be seriously interested in the wines and Thomas gives her a bundle of tasting notes, technical details and prices. With a flourish, he adds his card to the pile of literature. She picks it up and examines it. "Thanks," she says. "Sorry I haven't got any of my cards with me. But I'll pass this on to my colleague who handles Bordeaux. It's just a shame it isn't Gina any more these days."

He passes me a card as well. "Give us a ring any time if we can be of assistance with your studies."

It's very pleasant indeed sitting on this beautiful terrace talking to these knowledgeable and charming men, but reluctantly I realise it's half past seven and they will no doubt all be wanting to get home to their families and their Friday night suppers. Cédric has been quite quiet during the course of the evening, listening to the Cortinis as they talk about their wines, and occasionally asking Robert about his work in the vines or enquiring after his family. Their easy friendship is obvious though and they hug again fondly when we say goodbye. Old Monsieur Cortini plants enthusiastic kisses on the cheeks of his female guests and urges us to come and visit him again whenever we feel like it.

Cédric drops us back at the house, declining our offer of a further drink. "*Merci*, but we're having supper at my mother's house tonight. Another time perhaps though," he says. And do I imagine it, or is the look he gives me especially tender?

Obviously I don't imagine it as, the minute he's gone, Annie turns to me with a gleeful grin."Well, you've certainly made a huge impression there, Gina Peplow. He couldn't take his eyes off you all evening!"

"Old Monsieur Cortini, you mean? Yes, well I am particularly attractive to septuagenarians even if I do say so myself," I say in a vain attempt to deflect her.

"Bollocks Gina, you know I'm talking about Cédric. He's besotted with you. He went to all that trouble to take us over there and bring us back. He didn't need to be there at all. Probably just looking for an excuse to throw his awful harpy of a wife off the scent and spend an evening with you!"

"Don't say that," I wail in despair. "She's truly, honestly not like that at all. She's really lovely. I don't know what's going on, but I have to say I actually think the less of him for it. Honestly, what hope is there if even the most decent-seeming, well-thought-of, caring men behave like this?

"I'm sick of it all," I continue bitterly, working myself up to a fury that surprises even myself. "Lies, deception, cheating. It's grubby and hurtful and... and wrong!" I finish up somewhat lamely.

And I realise I don't know whether I'm talking about my situation or my mother's, whether I'm angry at Cédric or at my father and Liz. But one thing's for sure, I can choose not to be part of anything like that. So that's what I'm going to do.

*

On the last night of her holiday, Annie takes me out to dinner at a restaurant on the banks of the river, looking back across the stretch of dark water in whose depths the lights of Sainte Foy gleam like a school of golden fish. As we walk in, a man at one of the tables stands up and says, "*Bonsoir*." It's Robert Cortini, who shakes hands and introduces us to his wife, Christine. "It's our wedding anniversary," he explains, "so we thought we'd treat ourselves."

"Congratulations," I reply. "Have a good evening." And we make our way to our table at the other side of the room, leaving them to their meal.

"Isn't it nice when you start recognising people when you are out and about?" says Annie. "You must really be starting to feel like you belong."

We settle down with the menu. Once the waiter has taken our orders and deposited a basket of bread on the table before us, along with the bottle of chilled white wine that we've chosen, Annie reaches over and takes my hand. "Gina," she says seriously, "we need to talk."

"Oh no," I say in mock despair, "are you breaking up with me?"

"Of course not, I'd never do that," she smiles. "But I am worried about you. You've stuck yourself away down here in the depths of France in that lonely house with only a cat for company. You're not sleeping. And you're not eating properly, you're getting far too thin. And I couldn't help but notice that casket on the table in the sitting-room. I know it's none of my business, but I've got a strong suspicion it's not for keeping your secret supply of Ferrero Rochers in. It's not healthy, you know Gina. Having some time on your own is no bad thing, but you seem to be cutting yourself off completely. I know it's hard for you to trust again after what that two-timing shithead Roddy did to you, but you're too young to turn yourself into a lonely cat-loving spinster with the remains of a dead person for company. Honestly, it's like something out of a Hitchcock movie, you're going to go potty and start murdering people. And don't expect me to come and stay again if you do.

"It's like I said before," she continues, "you've got to get back into the saddle. Get out there again and meet somebody. Why don't you come back to England? You can stay on my sofa-bed while you look for a job. I know it's not the easiest of times, but maybe I can help you find something in the wine trade. Or you could write, like your dad did."

"Oh Annie, that's really kind of you, but I'm honestly ok here. I want to get the Masters' course under my belt and the studying will keep me busy in the autumn, plus a few trips back to England along the way. And I really do need some space at the moment. There are a few things I need to get sorted out in my head. Yes, admittedly I do have my aunt's ashes in my sitting-room, but it's only until I decide what to do with them. I just need a bit of time."

She lets go of my hand to allow the waiter to put our starters down in front of us, and tucks in to an oyster, washing it down with an appreciative slurp of wine.

"Well, ok, I'm going to give you 'til Christmas. But if you aren't looking better by then – and if you still have mortal remains sitting on your coffee table – then I'm coming over here to forcibly remove you. Deal?"

"Deal," I say, laughing and holding my hands up in mock surrender. "Don't worry, I'll be fine."

"Well, in my opinion you'll be fine a lot faster if you have a bit of good old fashioned hot sex. I know, I know," she forestalls me as I try to interrupt, "I'm not saying it has to be with the gorgeous, perfectly compatible, thoroughly nice-seeming man who is obviously keen on you and whom you clearly like in return. Good grief, that would be making life far too easy, after all!"

"Apart from the very serious complication that he's married with children," I butt in.

"Well yes, there is that," she concedes with a sigh. "But what about Thomas Cortini? He seems to be unattached. Didn't you like him? You've got his number, phone him up and say you want to come and give his sales strategy the once over. Or you need him to explain the ins and outs of malolactic fermentation. Or you'll come and help him with his next bottling run. Whatever. Think up some spurious excuse and make a move. That's what I'd do in your shoes."

"Sssh, keep your voice down, his brother might hear," I hiss, with a nod across the room to where Robert and his wife are tucking into their main courses. "And anyway, I don't fancy Thomas Cortini," I protest.

"Don't you? I thought he was cute. But in any case that's not the point here. He may not necessarily be the one, but he may be able to introduce you to his other single friends. You have to make an effort Gina, because men aren't just going to come marching up your drive."

"Actually you're wrong there," I say with an airy wave of my hand. "Men seem to be always doing exactly that. Just not the right ones," I laugh. "But I do take your point and I promise I'll make an effort. Anyway, let's just enjoy our meal. Now, tell me, what's on the agenda for when you get back...?"

After our meal, we emerge into the warm night air and wander across the bridge spanning the broad river, making our way back to where I've left the car. We stop beside one of the tall pillars covered with ivy and baskets of coral-pink petunias and lean on the parapet to gaze at the gold-flecked water flowing beneath us.

"This is a beautiful place," murmurs Annie dreamily.

Perhaps it's the wine making me maudlin, but I'm suddenly overwhelmed by a feeling of loneliness. "Oh Annie, I'm going to miss you so much." I lean my head on her shoulder for a second. "Thank you for being such a good friend."

She puts an arm around me and we stand like that companionably for a few moments.

"*Bonne nuit*," says a quiet voice beside us and we pull apart and turn to see Robert and Christine Cortini who are walking across the bridge arm-in-arm.

"Good night," we say. "We hope you had a good evening."

They nod and smile, continuing on their way, and we follow in their wake a few minutes later, driving home, under a sky filled with stars, in comfortable silence.

Chapter 12.

The house is very quiet after Annie's gone, leaving behind her a pile of sun-crinkled, suntan lotion-smudged magazines and a faint whiff of her Kenzo Amour perfume.

The August heat continues day after day and, despite the odd rumble of thunder carried on the thick night-time air now and then, there's no rain. By the end of the month even the vines are starting to look parched, the green rows dusty and a few leaves starting to bleach and fall. It's perfect weather for finishing off the ripening of the black Merlot and Cabernet Sauvignon grapes though, concentrating the flavours and sweetness into the promise of a full-blooded, heady vintage.

I've grown so used to the quiet company of just an old black cat and my own thoughts that I jump out of my skin when the chirp of the telephone suddenly breaks the silence one morning, almost tripping over the threshold as I dash inside to answer it.

It's Cédric.

Although sadly he's not calling to say that Marie-Louise has left him and would I like to move in. (I know, I know. Sorry, but I've got far too much time on my hands right now and it's bloody lonely. So yes, I admit I have whiled away the odd hour indulging in various highly unlikely fantasy solutions to my rapidly-encroaching spinsterhood.) I try to calm my breathing – panting is distinctly un-cool, after all. And I'm only out of breath as a result of my run to the phone, honest.

I smile into the handset, expecting Cédric to say he and Pierre will be along tomorrow to finish putting up the plasterboard. And so I'm disproportionately disappointed to hear him explain that Raphael has had an accident and they won't be able to come for several more weeks as they are now busy covering other jobs.

"I'm SO sorry," I say with heart-felt sincerity. "I hope Raphael is OK. Was it serious?"

"A stone fell and landed on his hand. An occupational hazard in our line of work. He has a broken wrist and two fingers were quite badly crushed. But he's tough and it'll mend. It's going to take a while though and we're very behind with several jobs that we need to get finished before the autumn. I'm very sorry Gina, but we have to prioritise. If you like I can give you the number of a plasterer who might be able to come and finish the work for you sooner."

"That's OK," I reply. "It's not urgent after all. I'll wait until you can do it if that's alright." And I'd rather have you in my bedroom than anyone else, I don't add.

"Once the weather changes we'll have more time for indoor work. I'll call you. And I really am sorry Gina."

Not half as sorry as I am, I think as I put down the phone. I wander back out to the terrace and pick up my book, the enticingly entitled "Concepts of Wine Technology", whose complicated chemical formulae I have, quite literally, been sweating over.

I sigh and put the book straight back down again, feeling disappointed and disgruntled.

And then a small rectangle of card that I've been using as a bookmark catches my eye. Thomas Cortini.

I hear Annie's voice urging me to call him up on some pretext or other. My heart's not really in it, but the prospect of the empty weeks stretching away before me suddenly makes me crave company. I look up, gazing absently at the view beyond the garden. Of course! The harvest is rapidly approaching, judging by the darkly ripe grapes on the vines all around me. I'll volunteer my services as an extra pair of hands. Despite my career in the world of wine, I've never actually worked a harvest. This is the perfect opportunity to learn a whole lot more about the detailed intricacies of winemaking first-hand. And it should be far more interesting seeing it done for real rather than trying to read about it in a book.

"Gina, how good to hear from you." Thomas' voice is genuinely warm. "How are you? Annie has returned to England now I suppose? You must be missing her. The harvest? Why yes, if the current weather holds we'll be starting on the whites next week or the week after. It's been so hot and dry the grapes are slightly small, but in wonderful condition and with very concentrated sugars. This year's challenge – and there always is one in winemaking as you know – is going to be managing the alcohol levels. But flavour-wise we're hoping for great things. We'd be delighted to have another pair of hands in the *chai*. I'll call you when we have a confirmed date, but *en principe* it'll be a week next Monday."

*

I'm surprised at how cold it is at six-thirty in the morning. Until now the days have still been beautifully warm, but then I'm not usually up this early. I nip back into the house and grab a fleece jacket before jumping into the car and driving to the Château de la Chapelle to report for duty. "Come about seven o'clock," Thomas instructed me yesterday. I'm early, eager to create a good impression on my first day. As I drive into the yard, I'm surprised to find it already a hive of activity.

The vast doors of the winery stand open and the bright lights inside throw a sharply-defined rectangle of illumination onto the white dust before the entrance. A conveyor belt has been positioned just inside and at the far end the de-stemming machine waits, silent for the moment. A pump sits underneath it and a long stainless steel tube runs from here to the top of one of the lofty metal tanks. Thomas and his father, perched on the metal walkway suspended above the *cuves*, are heaving the far end of the heavy pipe into position above the vat's open lid.

"Ah, here is our beautiful helper. *Bonjour* Mademoiselle Gina!" calls Patrick and he picks his way down the ladder-like stairs to come and greet me. Thomas follows behind him, having fixed the pipe in place.

"Gina, thank you for coming to help," he smiles. "Let me introduce you to Jacqueline, our assistant in the *chai*." A stocky, cheerful-looking young woman emerges from the office carrying a cardboard box under one arm and a gallon drum of yellow liquid. She sets these down and shakes my hand. A gleaming golden tooth embellishes her friendly grin, giving her a faintly piratical air.

"Enzymes and sulphites," she explains with a nod towards the containers. "You can help me make up the dilutions if you like."

She picks up the heavy plastic drum again with deceptive ease, and I grab the cardboard box and trot behind her to the sink in the corner of the *chai*. Jacqueline shows me how to mix a small carton of powdered enzyme with water in a two litre jug and then how to measure a tiny amount of the potent yellow liquid into a second jug, topping it up with water from the tap to dilute it. I struggle to understand her instructions through her thick south-western accent, and choke and splutter as I inhale some of the sulphurous vapour which burns my lungs and makes my eyes stream. "Careful," Jacqueline laughs, "the sulphites are powerful!" I gasp and nod, fumbling in my pocket for a tissue. "We add only a tiny amount," she explains. "The sulphites stabilise the grapes and the enzyme helps get the fermentation started. We'll feed these in very slowly as the first load arrives. Whoops, here he comes now..."

A tractor pulling a large, deep-sided trailer behind it swings into the yard and I glimpse Robert at the wheel. He reverses neatly, precision-perfect as he lines up the back of the trailer with the end of the conveyor belt.

"Come on," says Jacqueline. "We're on the sorting table. You stand on that side."

Robert jumps down from his cab and opens a round hatch in the end of the trailer while Jacqueline attaches a plastic pipe to an outlet on the underside to capture the juice that is already starting to run from the bunches of golden-green grapes. Catching sight of me, Robert comes round to say hello, then reaches back into the cab of the tractor to flick a switch. The trailer's internal screw mechanism begins to turn, disgorging its load in a steady stream onto the belt which Jacqueline has set running. She hits a button on the de-stemmer and another on the pump and the machinery leaps into action with an ear-splitting din.

Thomas appears at my side. "Take out any large sticks and leaves, and any bunches of grapes that don't look good," he shouts above the noise. I nod, concentrating hard on the moving belt before me and trying to pick though the heaps of fruit as nimbly as the other two. I find it hard to follow the fast-moving stream and rapidly begin to feel queasy with the movement and the noise and the fact that I didn't really feel like eating any breakfast at such an early hour this morning.

Jacqueline grins across at me, waving a hand to attract my attention. "Gina, are you OK? You've gone as white as a sheet. Don't try to follow the motion of the belt. Fix your gaze on one point, like this. That's better, you'll find it easier now."

Actually there isn't much debris to remove at all. The grapes are beautifully ripe, with no signs of mildew or rot and there are just a few leaves and the occasional woody bit of vine to take out. The bunches of fruit then fall through the de-stemmer which spits the stems into a bin, the loosened grapes pouring into the hopper of the pump where they are seized by the machinery and fired through the long pipe into the gaping mouth of the vat.

At last the stream of fruit coming out of the trailer dwindles and then stops and Robert nimbly switches off the screw, shuts the hatch and disconnects the hose from underneath, before hopping back into the cab and driving off for the next load. The last grapes drop into the pump and

Thomas hits the off-switch on the machinery, leaving us standing in sudden silence, the only sounds the soft dripping of juice into the vat and the ringing in my ears.

"Let me show you the control panel for the *cuves*," offers Thomas, leading the way to an efficient-looking array of lights and buttons fixed to the *chai* wall. "Five years ago we replaced our old *cuves* with thermo-regulated stainless steel ones, so we can control the temperature in each from here. The white grapes need to be kept cool to preserve the very delicate flavours of the fruit - that's why we start picking them so early, before the sun begins to warm them up – so we're chilling the vat they're going into. We're starting with the Sauvignon Blanc and it's vital to keep the grapes cool if you want to try to catch those elusive elderflower and gooseberry notes in the final wine. We'll easily finish the Sauvignon this morning and then change over vats to begin the Sémillon."

I nod. "Who's picking the grapes?" I ask.

"We use a local contractor, Benoît Michel. All our grapes are machine harvested nowadays. The technology is so good now it doesn't harm the vines the way some of the old *vendangeurs* used to. And this way we can get our grapes in at the very best moment when they reach optimum ripeness. So we have two people working in the vines today, Benoît driving the *vendangeur* and Robert bringing in the trailer loads of fruit. The turnaround is very efficient."

And right on cue we hear the tractor manoeuvring the next trailer into position at the end of the sorting table. We hurry back to our positions as the stream of green-gold fruit starts to pour onto the conveyer belt and the machinery roars into action once again.

Two trailer loads later, Christine Cortini appears in the *chai* doorway, a large wicker basket over one arm. She does the rounds, greeting each of us in turn and then busies herself in the office. A delicious aroma of percolating coffee wafts in our direction. Suddenly I realise how cold my hands and feet are from standing on the cement floor at the sorting table, my fingers and the cuffs of my sleeves stickily damp with a mixture of chilly grape juice and dew. The last of the batch of grapes trundles along the conveyor belt, then rattles into the de-stemmer and the fruit cascades into the pump. Jacqueline nips round to hit the off-buttons on the machines and gestures towards the office with a tilt of her head. "Coffee time."

I rinse my hands and then rub my neck, which is beginning to ache, trying to roll the stiffness out of my shoulders. I glance at my watch. It's not even ten o'clock and I feel like I've done a good day's work already.

Christine is pouring strong, hot coffee into cups and hands me one. "Sugar?" she offers, pushing a box of sugar lumps towards me. I clasp my hands around the small cup to warm them, wishing it was a large British mug with a generous slug of hot milk added. But in my cold, tired state the shot of scalding, tarry liquid is the best cup of coffee I've ever drunk. The men come in from the vines, Benoît shaking hands all round, and the whole team stands around the desk drinking coffee and munching flaky croissants which Christine produces from her basket. Patrick, who has been everywhere this morning, darting from sorting table to trailer to *cuve*, and even popping out into the vines to supervise activities there, is euphoric about the quality of this year's harvest. "A wonderful year, even better than 2005, you'll see. Gina, you'll be able to boast to your friends that you have had a hand in making some of the finest wines of the century!"

"And the century is not even ten years old yet," remarks Thomas drily.

"It is going to be an outstanding year though," says Benoît, (another thick *sud-ouest* accent for me to try to decipher). "Especially for the reds. I've never seen such clean Merlot. And the Cabernet Sauvignon is going to be superb. Perfectly ripe."

"Yes, as long as we don't get thunderstorms next week," says Robert shaking his head. "A downpour at this stage and in this heat can rot the grapes overnight. With the sudden rain they can swell and split," he explains to me. "You can even get hail sometimes, which is disastrous. All that work and care throughout the year and then you can lose the whole lot just before the harvest. *Vignerons* don't sleep well at the best of times, and at this time of year hardly at all."

"Pah!" exclaims Patrick, "don't you worry we'll get the harvest in alright. And just you wait and see. It's the vintage of the century I tell you! Right, back to work everyone."

Robert already has another trailer-load of grapes waiting for us, so we get straight back down to it. Revived by the break, I sort the fruit with new energy and am gratified to notice that my fingers are now working almost as fast as Jacqueline's across from me. The coffee has warmed me up and the sun is now starting to heat the air outside the entrance. We work on cheerfully for another hour and then the rhythm of our work is broken as Robert announces that that's the Sauvignon Blanc finished and they're about to start bringing in the Sémillon.

As he drives off with the trailer, there's a flurry of activity in the *chai*. We have to change over to another *cuve*, which involves re-positioning the huge metal pipe. Thomas nimbly climbs up onto the walkway in the roof and manhandles the top end, while Jacqueline and I wrestle with the bottom. There are a series of joints in the piping, each closed with a strong metal clip and we have to release these to swing the steel tubing round to reach the new vat. I strain to undo one clip, scraping my fingers and breaking a couple of nails, while Jacqueline competently manages the others. We get the pipe into position just in time as Robert arrives with the next trailer-load.

"Quick, the sulphites and enzymes," calls Jacqueline. I run to the sink to make up the new concoctions. In my haste I slop some of the searing yellow liquid down the side of the jug and gasp as my nose, eyes and lungs burn, before discovering that gasping is the worst thing to do. My face streaked with tears, I hurry back to the sorting table with the two heavy jugs of liquid treatments. The belt is already running as Jacqueline takes them from me, and I wipe my eyes on my sleeve so that I can focus on the fast-moving stream of grapes.

On the dot of midday, silence falls again as Thomas switches off the machines. We've filled one tall vat with Sauvignon Blanc and half filled its neighbour with larger, yellower Sémillon grapes. "Lunchtime," says Jacqueline with gusto. "Christine cooks for everyone during harvest so it'll be good. It's on the terrace."

In the loo I catch sight of my reflection in the mirror with horror. My nose is red and my face shiny from sulphur-induced tears. My hair is wild, coming out of the elastic I've tied it back with and sticking out in strange wisps where I must have pushed it back with hands covered in grape juice, a natural but not very becoming alternative to hair gel. I wash my hands and face and let my hair down, tucking the band into my pocket for later. As we step out onto the terrace, I blink in the midday sunlight and peel off my jacket to let the rays warm my aching shoulders. At a trestle table set with a checked cloth, Christine is setting out baskets of bread and plates of pâté. Suddenly I realise I'm absolutely ravenous, despite the mid-morning croissant.

"*Bon appétit*," smiles Christine as she pulls up a chair. Patrick pulls the corks from two bottles of Clairet and tours the table, filling glasses with the pomegranate-coloured wine.

Thomas offers me the basket of bread and I smear a crusty chunk of baguette with rich, garlicky pâté. "How have you enjoyed your first morning?" he asks.

I chew and swallow. "Good," I reply. "Hard work, but I was expecting that, and very interesting. It's great feeling you're part of the process that leads to something as wonderful as this." I raise my glass. "And I still find it a magical process. You take all those trailer-loads of grapes and turn them into bottles of wine. It's a kind of alchemy."

Thomas smiles. "You're right. Even after all these years we still find it miraculous too. And you never really know what you're going to end up with until the final blending and bottling. There's a saying around here that red wine is made on the vine and white wine is made in the *chai*. Each has its own particular challenges."

Robert chips in from the other side of the table, "Yes. This year we've been lucky with the weather, but there's still lots to do before the wine is in the bottles and we can start to relax a little." He starts to tick items off on his fingers. "There's the initial fermentation, then the malo-lactic fermentation, pumping over the reds to extract all the flavours from the skins, pressing just enough to balance the tannins, fining and filtering, and all the time carefully moving all those hectolitres of liquid from *cuve* to press, to barrel, to bottle without letting the air oxidise the wine. I wish it were just as easy as waving a magic wand."

"Fortunately we also have the expertise of a really good oenologist, Sylvie Clemenceau," adds Thomas. "Christine will drop off samples from today's *cuves* at the lab this afternoon and Sylvie will come by tomorrow to confirm sugar levels and advise us on how to get the best out of this year's harvest. I'll introduce you when she comes. She'll be a good contact for you if you need help with any of the more technical details."

Patrick is now handing round a platter of pork chops and he deposits a huge slab of the golden, fragrant meat on my plate. "Here you are Gina, we need to feed you up ready for a hard afternoon's work." Christine follows in his wake, cradling a steaming bowl of fried potatoes, encrusted with dark flecks of sweet-smelling garlic, in a tea-towel. I pile my plate high. I'm certainly not going to lose any weight during this stint of work-experience. A green salad moistened with the tang of mustard vinaigrette follows and then a white wheel of creamy camembert. The last crusts of bread are used to wipe plates clean, as Christine pours us each a small black coffee to round off the meal. I drink mine thankfully, needing an antidote to the comfortable blanket of drowsiness the food, wine and sun are weaving over me.

Suddenly I hear the words "... Thibault *frères*..." and I tune in to a conversation Robert and Christine are having with Benoît and Jacqueline.

"Marie-Louise says Raphael's hand is still quite bad," says Christine. "It's taking a long time for the break to mend. But it doesn't stop him turning up on site to tell them they're not doing the job right!" The others chuckle appreciatively.

"What are they working on at the moment?" asks Jacqueline.

"The church at Les Lèves," replies Robert. "They won the contract to re-do all the stonework, including the bell-tower. It's a massive job. Short-handed as they are, they're going to battle to finish it on time. They're working straight through every weekend at the moment."

Benoît whistles through his teeth. "Have you seen the scaffolding they've had to put up? Took them nearly a week just to do that. And the quality of the stonework is amazing. Each new stone for the bell-tower has to be cut individually and some of the detail's very fancy."

Robert agrees. "Yes, we think maintaining a vineyard is hard work. But working with stone like that and at such heights, now that's what I call a tough job."

Suddenly my bedroom ceiling seems a complete embarrassment. I now appreciate fully what a favour Cédric and his brothers have done me. And how much clout their diminutive mother must have over her strapping sons to have persuaded them to help me out in the first place. I'm beginning to wish I'd taken up Cédric's offer of the contact details of a plasterer. I'm quite sure finishing off the work on my roof is a complete nuisance for them and they're just too polite to say so – or too afraid of Mireille. I keep quiet, feeling rather ashamed, and take another sip of my coffee. The others down theirs and push back their chairs.

Robert and Benoît leave the table first, heading back out into the vines for the next load. Back in the *chai* the sides of the two steel vats we've been filling are now covered in droplets of condensation up to the level of the cooling grapes and juice within. We work on steadily and by five o'clock we've filled three *cuves* with white grapes.

"Good work," enthuses Patrick as he inspects the temperature control panel's winking lights.

"We'll get the Sémillon finished tomorrow and probably the Muscadelle too – there's very little of that. We'll get started on the pressing in the afternoon. *Alors*, let's get everything cleared away.

At the end of the long day I'm bone-achingly tired. The restorative effects of lunch have worn off long ago and there's been no stopping for a British-style tea break in the afternoon. And now we have to hose down the equipment, taking apart the de-stemming machine and rinsing every grape skin and stalk out of its honeycombed drum. Then we clean the pump and all the tubing, spewing residue onto the *chai* floor. This then has to be scraped up using a long-handled rubber blade, known as a *raclette*, and shovelled into bins. Finally the cement floor has to be hosed down and the water scraped into the drain that runs down the centre of the *chai*. Finally, at six o'clock, peace falls as Jacqueline turns off the pressure sprayer and I scrape away the last drops of water.

"Impeccable," declares Patrick.

I am now so tired I can hardly speak. I ache all over and my head feels heavy and dull from trying to follow the rapid-fire colloquial French spoken by my colleagues in such strong accents. I'm cold and damp and hungry.

It's the best day I've had in ages.

"Goodbye Gina, I hope we haven't put you off winemaking forever," smiles Thomas.

"Not a bit," I reply. "See you tomorrow. Seven a.m?"

Chapter 13.

The first week of the harvest passes in a blur.

The white grapes are all picked in the first two days and then Benoît disappears with his harvesting machine – a massive beast of a contraption – to work at another château for a few days. The green grapes macerate briefly in their own pale golden juice in the stainless steel vats before we pump them out, through more heavy lengths of piping, into the big yellow press. Thomas flicks the controls to exactly the right setting, to extract as much precious juice as possible from the fruit without over-crushing the skins and pips with their strong, teeth-furring tannins that could easily overpower the delicate flavours. The cloudy juice is then fed back into another *cuve* and left to get on with the serious business of fermentation.

Jacqueline and I toil to shovel the leftover skins into a sizeable heap on the hardstand in front of the *chai*, which is picked up at the end of each day by a lorry, doing the rounds of the local wineries to take the must to the state-run distillery. "Yet another tax we have to pay to the government here in France," grumbles Patrick when I ask him about it.

Then, arms and back aching from this surprisingly heavy spadework, it's time to clean the *chai* again. Everything has to be kept scrupulously clean to avoid contaminating the wines and ensure that the tiny, innocent-looking flies that could turn a whole vat into vinegar, are kept at bay.

As soon as the whites have been pressed, Benoît reappears with the *vendangeur* to begin harvesting the Merlot and then, finally, the Cabernet Sauvignon. And so it's back out with the sorting table again as the blue-black grapes begin to pour from the back of Robert's trailer.

The white grapes were just a gentle introductory ripple, it turns out, compared to the tsunami of reds. The levels in the tall vats rise like an inexorable purple tide.

First we fill *cuves* for making Clairet, the fruit macerating for just a few days to allow the juice to take on some of the flavours from the grapes, as well as a glorious sunrise tinge from the colour in the skins.

The red wines will be allowed to macerate thoroughly, with the juice being carefully pumped over the thick, solid cap of skins that forms on the top, in order to keep extracting the flavours and tannins from the Merlot and Cabernet Sauvignon grapes. And they will ferment before they're pressed, unlike the more rapid turnaround of the whites and the Clairet.

We fill tank after tank, the only pauses coming when it's time to wrestle the cumbersome metal piping from one *cuve* to the next. Some of the Merlot vinestocks are very old – "Sixty years or more, planted by my grandfather," says Patrick proudly – and with these grapes comes considerably more debris to be picked out on the sorting table. My hands fly, adept now, as I turn over piles of fruit to pull out sticks and leaves. Occasionally a tiny, emerald-green frog - a *reinette,* Jacqueline tells me – has to be rescued before being carried on the swiftly flowing tide of grapes into the de-stemming machine. And Thomas and Jacqueline burst out laughing when I let out an involuntary shriek as I reach for a chunk of brown stick that suddenly darts across my hand and scuttles across the floor back into the sunshine: a lizard with a tale to tell its relatives back in the vines.

The highlight of each day is the lunch break when we all gather on the terrace for another of Christine's delicious, and apparently effortlessly prepared, meals. It's not just the good food and the welcome chance to sit down in the sun-dappled warmth for an hour or so. I find myself slowly starting to feel included, a fellow-worker and one of the team rather than just a curious foreigner who's popped along to play at winemaking for a day or two. I've tuned in to the personalities of the group and the rhythm of the work in the *chai* and no longer feel like a clumsy outsider as I learn the steps to the whirling waltz of the wine harvest. Finally, instead of just reading about it in books, I'm joining in the dance.

Each night I soak my aching limbs in a hot bath and then collapse wearily into bed. Once I was so tired I even fell asleep in the tub, the cooling water jerking me back to consciousness as it lapped around my stiffening shoulders. And I sleep better than I have done in ages. The combination of physical labour, hearty meals and stimulating company is a healthier diet than I've had for a long time.

*

The unmistakeable scent of fermentation begin to percolate through the *chai*, a fruity yeastiness that hints at the extraordinary changes that are taking place in the vats of grape juice. And most days Sylvie Clemenceau, the oenologist, comes by to discuss the results of the latest tests that have been carried out on samples from each of the *cuves*. Patrick and Thomas call me over the first day she arrives.

I take to her immediately. Her wide brown eyes and mop of curly hair accompany a smile as warm as the early autumn sunshine outside the *chai* door. Her manner tells of a quiet competence, as she patiently explains each step of the testing process and the results for my benefit.

"So it's as we would expect after such a hot summer, the sugar levels are very high, which is going to translate to higher alcohol levels in the wine than normal. Rather like many reds from the New World that are grown in hot, sunny climates. There's also a greater risk of the fermentation stopping before it's complete so we'll have to watch for that. We may need to use different yeast. We will need to filter later on. And we'll probably add a little more of the press wine than usual to the free-run. That will increase the tannins as they are quite mellow this year with the ripeness of the grapes. The blending is going to be critical to make sure we get the balance right."

"Fortunately Gina has an excellent palate," says Thomas. "We'll include you when it comes to the blending stage," he says turning to me, "although of course that'll only take place in the spring once the malolactic fermentation has occurred."

"In the meantime," offers Sylvie, "if you'd like to come and spend a morning with me in the lab you'd be very welcome. I can show you exactly how the samples are tested and how we obtain and record the results."

"I'd love to," I reply. "That'll be a huge help in trying to understand some of the chemistry." I turn to Patrick and Thomas. "If the Cortinis can spare me, that is?"

Patrick smiles. "Well it'll be a loss, but we'll let you have a morning off once we start pressing the Clairet. We'll have finished the Merlot then and we're going to wait a couple of days longer before we bring in the Cabernet Sauvignon. For once, the weather is on our side this year."

*

And so a few days later I present myself at the little laboratory opposite the Mairie in Saint André-et-Appelles for a morning's apprenticeship. It's a very different place of work, a tiny pair of rooms with clinical white walls, although everything is as scrupulously, almost surgically clean as the equipment in the *chai*. When I arrive, Sylvie is talking to a winemaker who has come to hand in some samples. "Come on through," she says once he has departed, and she shows me to the little lab behind the reception room. Crates of sample bottles are stacked high, each one neatly labelled. "As you can see, it's very important to be systematic and to make a careful note of where each sample is from," she says. "Imagine how disastrous it would be if we gave the wrong results back."

She hands me a white coat. "Here, put this on. Now you look the part. We'll make a chemist of you yet!"

"Thanks," I say, "but I think it's going to take more than a white coat to achieve that."

We perch on stools at a long counter and Sylvie shows me how she carries out the basic tests. "For more complex analysis we send the samples to the main lab at Sauveterre," she explains. "The turnaround is fast and we can have the results back to each *vigneron* the same day."

We are interrupted at regular intervals as more samples are dropped off and at eleven o'clock the driver arrives to collect the batches for taking to the Sauveterre laboratory.

We pause then for a welcome coffee break. While it's less physically tiring than working in the *chai*, I'm finding it mentally exhausting trying to keep track of the stream of information Sylvie is imparting. I scribble notes frantically. But light is beginning to dawn and it's already far clearer seeing the chemistry in action than my attempts to understand it from the textbooks.

"So that covers the main tests we do at this stage in the winemaking process," Sylvie summarises, ticking off on her fingers the tests for sugar content, phenols, alcohol levels and problems such as mildew and grey mould. "We'll test for volatile acids if necessary after the first fermentation has occurred. And of course the other main round of testing we do is in the spring, to establish whether or not malolactic fermentation has taken place. Let me show you how we do that to give you an idea. I think I have some old duplicate results." She pulls open the drawer of a filing cabinet and extracts a folder.

"Ah yes, here we are. We use paper chromatography to carry out this test. As you know, we need to make sure that the malic acid has been transformed into softer lactic acid and this happens during a second fermentation, which may occur in the tank or after the wine has been put into barrels." She hands me two squares of textured white paper. "Can you spot the difference?"

I ponder the purple-brown stains on each of the sheets, fading in a spectrum as the paper, exposed to a chemical solvent, has separated out the different constituents of the wine as they soaked their way up to the top of the paper. Finally I point to the right hand one. "This one has a gap, just here," I say.

"Exactly right," replies Sylvie. "What it is showing is an absence of malic acid, which is still present on the other sheet, here you see? So that is how we know the second fermentation has taken place. We test for something that isn't there, rather than something that is. In other words, we're looking for a negative."

And suddenly, triggered by her words, my mind catapults off at a complete tangent. Why didn't I think of it before? A negative. There has to be one. Of the photo of my father. And maybe there'll be others too. Images that will give me more of a clue about the extent and timing of their relationship. Pieces of the nightmarish jigsaw that I'm trying to put together, with most of the bits missing and no idea of the final picture. I can hardly concentrate on the rest of what Sylvie is saying and am relieved when the hands of the clock nudge round to midday and it's lunchtime.

"Thanks very much Sylvie, it was a wonderful morning, so helpful," I say as I leave.

"Well I'll see you back at Château de la Chapelle before too long," she replies. "I'll be popping back in the next few days no doubt."

"See you," I wave as I get into my car and head up the hill for home. I don't have to be back at the Cortinis' until after lunch. Lafite, who's been curled up peacefully on a chair in the kitchen, looks up startled as I crash through the door, flinging my keys onto the table.

I head straight through to the study. Liz's files are arranged in one of the big bookcases that line the walls, each neatly labelled by year. Within them, alphabetical dividers separate plastic sleeves which hold strips of negatives, each marked with a small white sticker giving the name of the subject and the precise date the photos were taken. I work feverishly, going first to the folder for 1972, the year of my birth. I start with the obvious, (which would be making things just too simple of course, but I live in hope), turning to 'P' for Peplow and then 'D' for David. I leaf through the plastic sleeves but find nothing. I need to think more laterally. I turn to 'W' for wine. There are several strips of pictures of wine bottles and barrels, but no picture of my father tagged on to one of these as an afterthought. 1973 is the same. Next I seize the folder marked 1971, the year my parents met, the year of their wedding. I'm certain Liz and Dad didn't meet before this, my mother told me so categorically when I asked why Liz wasn't in the wedding photos, so this is the very earliest year from which the photo could date. I page through again, squinting as I hold strips of negatives up to the light to make sure none of the figures is Dad.

Liz was a professional. She methodically and systematically catalogued every picture she took. Even ones that turned out badly are still here, though they've been scored through with a marking pen. Some of them are amazing. Pictures of fashion models and portraits of film stars leap out at me. But none is the photo I'm looking for. Finally, just as I'm about to give up, I page through the 1971 folder and turn randomly to 'V'. And there it is. 'Vins, Salon, Bordeaux. 22-24 Oct 1971' in Liz's neat handwriting. I pull out the three strips of negatives, holding each up to the window to scrutinise them in the light. There are figures in many of the pictures, but none is my father. I start to slide the strips of film back into their transparent sleeves. And then I stop. Each frame is numbered with its own tiny digits. And between two of the strips, three numbers are missing. I check back through the other pages of negatives. All the numbers are there. It's only on the strip I'm holding in my trembling fingers that three of the frames have been carefully cut off. And I realise I have a result.

Just like the test at the lab, sometimes you have to look for what is missing.

The acid test for a guilty conscience.

*

My insomnia is back with a vengeance. I've spent the afternoon working in the *chai*, where Jacqueline and I had to attach the pipes and pumps to six full *cuves* of Merlot and pump the juice over the cap of skins in each one. I've lugged equipment to and fro and run up and down the catwalk's steep metal stairs countless times to readjust pipes over the top of the vats. I've wheeled a heavy canister of carbon dioxide gas from one end of the winery to the other while Jacqueline carefully topped up the tanks of whites, so that no air can come into contact with the wine causing it to oxidise. And I've helped wrestle into place the lengths of steel piping to carry the contents of the vats of Clairet to the press, causing a minor disaster when, distracted by the thought of those missing negatives, (what *was* Dad doing in the other two pictures?), I accidentally undid one of the joints too early, flooding the floor of the *chai* with sticky pink juice, pips and skins. Clearing up took even longer than usual this evening.

I was too preoccupied to eat any lunch and too distracted to eat supper. Lafite's indignant, hungry meowing finally made me put away the files that I had spread about the study floor, kneeling in the middle of them and looking for more missing negatives. But it seems Liz didn't go to any more Salons des Vins. I could find no similar entries in subsequent folders.

So now my head aches from squinting at negatives, my stomach is growling with hunger and yet again I'm wide awake at two a.m., my mind buzzing. What have I learned? That the photo of Dad was very probably taken either during or immediately after the wine exhibition in October 1971. Meaning that he'd been married to Mum for about four months. And I would be born eight months later, on the 15th June, 1972.

I wonder again whether this means Liz was really my mother, picturing the scenario where Mum agreed to raise the baby, the result of a moment of madness between her husband and her sister. Could she have faked those photos in the album at home? Surely not. And certainly not that Caesarian scar. I turn over in bed and thump the pillow in annoyance, trying to make a more comfortable cushion for my pounding head.

The good thing, small consolation though it may be, is that it looks as if maybe they didn't spend time together again. Although I realise there's no evidence for this. Maybe she just stopped taking photos of him after the first time...

I think of the urn of Liz's ashes, still on the coffee table in the sitting room. I'm no nearer to deciding what to do with it. But tomorrow I'm going to shut the door so I don't have to look at it every time I go past. Ha! That'll teach her. Though of course it won't.

Troubled, broken dreams blur the boundaries between wakefulness and sleep, a shifting kaleidoscope of faces and photographs. I'm in the *chai* with Dad and I give him a glass of wine to try from one of the vats. It's a wine I've made myself. I wait with pride, and some trepidation, to hear his verdict. "God Gina, this is absolutely dire," he says. "What have you done to it?" Furious, I take the glass and taste it myself. He's right. It's off. Sulphurous and stinking. Like wet dog and mouldy rubber. The liquid is murky and covered in slime, like water in a stagnant pond. I look around the *chai* and see Liz pressing buttons on the temperature control panel. "Hey!" I shout. "Get away from there!" She ignores me and the lights start to flash a warning, an electronic alarm beeping insistently. And I struggle up, surfacing through the layers of sleep to find my alarm going off because it's time to get up once again and go to work at Château de la Chapelle.

Chapter 14.

By the time the last of the Cabernet Sauvignon has been pressed, it's the middle of October. I've been working at Château de la Chapelle for four weeks and the harvest is now over. Across the region, only the occasional harvesting machine can still be seen sailing ponderously up and down the vineyard rows, bringing in the late-harvested Sémillon grapes at the chateaus where they make the sweet wines for which Monbazillac and Sauternes are famous. The bunches are furred with a blanket of noble rot and will be made into a golden nectar that is as mellow as the autumn sunlight.

The final job for us in the *chai* is to decant the fermented and pressed red wines carefully into barrels. Universally acknowledged as the best in the world, the wood comes from ancient forests in the middle of France. Englishmen may lay claim to hearts of oak, but France's heart truly is made of oak and each year she generously sacrifices a little to help finish off the wines that her sons and daughters have laboured so hard to create. The Cortinis replace about a third of their barrels each year, so Jacqueline and I are unwrapping the bulky, curved parcels that have been delivered from the barrel-maker. I love the smell of the wood and stroke the smooth fineness of its grain as I peel off the plastic covers. We roll the barrels into position in the cellar and wedge chocks under each one to hold it in place. Then, closely supervised by their father, Thomas and Robert connect up the pumps and pipes that will lead the wine from the vats into each *barrique*, where it will stay for up to a year while the deep red liquid is suffused with the smooth vanilla flavours from the wood, which help to add depth and balance to the mix of fruit and tannins.

Patrick gently knocks a silicone bung into the top of each barrel. These will be removed at regular intervals so that the levels can be kept topped up to prevent too much air getting in and spoiling the wine.

The barrels exude a delicate breath, filling the cellar with faint perfumes of fruits and flowers. The wines are shaping up nicely, but the Cortinis will only really know what this year's vintage will taste like when the time comes for the final blending next year.

"And now," says Patrick with a smile, "we breathe a sigh of relief and have a small pause."

"Yes," grins Thomas, "before we have to do it all over again."

"And of course in the meantime there's the small question of pruning the vines, replacing those that are damaged, replanting the areas that are past their best, ploughing and spraying," adds Robert. "Not to mention bottling, labelling and actually selling the wines..."

Patrick raises his bushy eyebrows and shrugs. "Ah *oui*, my dear sons, but that is business as usual. Whatever else could you possibly wish to be doing instead?"

*

In the vineyards bordering my garden, now that the fruit has been harvested the leaves turn a glorious gold, a final flourish before the vines transform themselves into black, wizened stumps for the winter. Magpies balance on the wooden posts that support the trellis of fine wires on which the vines are trained. Mostly the birds are in pairs, (oh joy!), but occasionally these coalesce into larger groups, fluttering and squabbling as each tries to assert its territorial rights. Distracted from my reading, I count them over and over again as the birds group and re-group and I try not to think of the photo in the silver frame.

At long last Cédric phones. To be honest, I've stopped wondering when he'll call. I've got used to lying in bed at night gazing blankly up at the silver-covered insulation and the rough laths of the roofing. I've pushed away any thoughts of attraction between us and just about managed to convince myself that I'm so focused on my MW studies now that there's no room for anything – or anyone – else in my life. So when I pick up the phone and hear his voice there's only the faintest quickening of my heartbeat, and I am pleased to note the air of calm detachment in my voice as I reply to his questions. Yes, I've been fine, yes, I enjoyed working the harvest at Château de la Chapelle, yes, the studies are coming on fine. And the work on the church at Les Lèves?

"Finished, thank goodness," he says. "You'll have to come and see it one of these days. It's turned out well we think. I'd be pleased to show you what we've done."

And Raphael's hand?

"Better now, he's back in action. He and Florian are finishing dismantling the scaffolding on the church tower. So Pierre and I can come on Monday morning to get started on the work on the ceiling for you, if that's convenient? We've got a couple of things we need to do in the afternoon, but we should be able to get the job finished on Tuesday morning at the latest. It's not going to take us long."

"Yes, that'd be fine" I reply. "But there's no rush. Come whenever suits you, if you have other work you need to get done first."

How cool am I?

"No, Monday will be fine. You've been very patient. We'll be there around nine. We need to go to Lacombe first to get the materials we'll need."

"OK, if you're sure. That's great then. Have a good weekend. Until Monday."

And I sit back down at my desk, feeling just a little wistful for something that's now over. Before it had ever even begun.

*

I'm still glad to see the blue pickup, closely followed by the red motorbike, roll up the drive on Monday morning. I've shut myself away from the outside world since the harvest, politely declining the occasional invitation from Celia to come for lunch or dinner, my only other human contact – apart from sporadic trips to the supermarket - my phone calls to my mother once a week and cheery emails from Annie full of news and jokes and how busy she is at work. My replies, in comparison, seem stilted and boring. So it's good to have Cédric and Pierre here, for a day or so at least, and to have some noise and activity in the house. Lafite winds himself round Cédric's green overall-clad legs and he crouches to stroke him.

Straightening up, he catches sight of me standing in the doorway and comes to kiss me on both cheeks. "Gina, it's good to see you again," he says warmly.

As he smiles, the lines around his eyes crinkle in a way that makes my heart lurch.

Honestly woman, get a grip. What is it about this man? I'm absolutely resolved not to waste any more time on impossible, unattainable relationships and I reply briskly, with a brightness that sounds brittle to my ears.

"Lovely to see you both. Come on in. You know the way..."

They bring in tools, sections of a small scaffolding platform and large sheets of grey plasterboard and carry everything upstairs. I've managed to push the bed into a corner away from the open area of ceiling that they'll be working on. They quickly cover everything in clean plastic sheeting and set to work.

I feel more light-hearted than I have done in weeks as I hear the two men chatting and laughing easily as they work in the room above me. It's just that it's nice having company in the house, I tell myself cheerily. Even if I am paying for it to be here, I think, rather more glumly.

At midday they come down the stairs. "Well, we've got the boards up," says Cédric. "I'll pop back tomorrow morning to tape the joints and skim them and then the ceiling will be ready for you to paint. We'll leave the scaffold platform here for you, it's much safer than a ladder. It's going to be as good as new when you've finished."

Pierre puts on his helmet and gives a wave as he roars off down the drive, leaving a cloud of white dust hanging in the air behind him.

Cédric busies himself putting tools into his pickup. Do I imagine it, or is he playing for time?

"We've left the bed in the corner for the time being," he says. "Otherwise we'd just have to move it again tomorrow. I hope that's OK?"

"Fine," I say.

"Gina," he says. And hesitates, suddenly awkward. "There's something I wanted to ask you."

He sounds nervous, something I've never heard in him before.

"Yes?" I ask. And suddenly I find I can't swallow because my throat has constricted. With hope? Or is it despair?

"If you aren't busy, would you come and have dinner with me tomorrow evening?"

A bombshell.

It's all I've ever wanted and all I don't. Handed to me on a plate after all these months of wondering, dreaming, hoping. He must see written clearly on my face the conflicting emotions that crowd in as I take on board what he is asking. What he is offering.

It's everything. And nothing at all.

I clear my throat. "Just to be clear," I say cautiously. "Who else would be there?"

He looks confused.

"Nobody. Just you and me. We can go wherever you like..."

As he tails off, a red rage floods my veins like liquid fire, flushing my face with its righteous heat.

"How dare you," I say, coldly but my voice is shaking with emotion. "What the hell is it with you Frenchmen? No, never mind you French, just men. You all think you can play games with women. The fact that someone is in a serious relationship seems to mean nothing at all to you. Well I can tell you, I'm not interested in cheating. I want no part of it. So thank you very much for your terribly kind invitation," I'm getting into my stride now and my voice is stronger, sarcastic, my French gratifyingly fluent, "but I don't think I want what you are offering. Affairs are just not my style."

He drops his eyes, ashamed. And so he should be. Poor Marie-Louise. Poor Nathalie and Luc.

"I'm... I'm sorry Gina," he stammers. "I didn't realise... I didn't think..."

"That I'd mind? Well I do. You picked the wrong girl I'm afraid. Sorry. Let's just not mention this again, OK?"

And I turn on my heel and stalk into the kitchen, firmly closing the door behind me.

Through the glass I see him climb into the cab of his truck, his shoulders sagging. He sits staring out through the windscreen for a few seconds before starting the engine and driving off. And I collapse into a chair and bury my fingers in my hair, clutching both sides of my head in anger. And not a little frustration. And, if I'm being perfectly honest, total disappointment and despair. If even Cédric, this quiet, strong, capable, warm, family-loving man wants to have his cake and eat it too, what hope is there for womankind?

I groan, reliving the scene that has just taken place, cringing with embarrassment and humiliation. How awkward is it going to be when he comes back tomorrow? If he comes back tomorrow – maybe he won't now and my bedroom ceiling will remain forever unfinished and I'll have to lie in my lonely, spinster bed every night and look up at it as a reminder of what could have been. Am I being a prude? Do other women merrily leap into bed with married men all the time? (At the drop of a hat. Or rather a pair of trousers.) How awkward is it going to be when I run into Mireille? Or, oh god, Marie-Louise?

What a disaster. And I'm never going to meet anyone living here. But I can't go back to England yet. Unless I sell the house. That's what I'll have to do. Who in their right mind would want to live here anyway? Where my father most probably betrayed my mother with her own sister. Where I've been coming all these years ignorant of that fact, thinking I loved this place, believing I was loved by my aunt. Now the tears are rolling down my face, and I let them come, crying until I am emptied out. And afterwards, spent and exhausted, I go upstairs and lie down on the bed in the corner of the bedroom and gaze blankly up at the neatly patched ceiling until I fall asleep.

*

I'm up early the next morning. I didn't sleep much anyway, inevitably. I'm determined to be brisk and businesslike when Cédric arrives. It's not going to take him long to finish up and I'm keen to get him out of both the house and my life as quickly as possible. I sit studiously at my computer, trying to convince myself - and anyone who should happen to come up the drive - that I'm terribly busy with some important research. The clock in the hall ticks ponderously and the minutes stretch to hours. No-one appears. Well, what did I expect? He's obviously gone off in a huff, his male ego wounded by my rejection, and now the ceiling's never going to be finished.

It's early afternoon when I hear the sound of an engine in the courtyard. I glance towards the window and the wind is taken out of my sails somewhat when I see it's Pierre's motorbike that's arrived instead of Céedric's pickup. I go to the door.

"Hello," I say politely.

Pierre is distant, preoccupied. "Hello Gina," he says. "I've come to finish things off. Sorry I couldn't get here this morning, Raphael needed me on another job. May I come in?" He shrugs a small rucksack off his shoulders.

"Of course."

We both sound stilted and self-conscious. Clearly he knows what's happened and has come in his brother's place, to save him any further embarrassment. Well at least Cédric must have a guilty conscience – that's something, I suppose.

Pierre busies himself upstairs, his silence a stark contrast to yesterday's cheerful banter. Apart from a somewhat stony request for water, with which to mix the filler that he's going to skim over the joints, there's no conversation. I try to concentrate on my work, but the atmosphere is as oppressive as the build up to a summer thunderstorm and my head feels hot and heavy. I push aside a pile of notebooks with a sigh. Honestly, why should I be made to feel like this? I'm the innocent one here. Who knows what Cédric has told his brother... Maybe he said I tried to make a pass at him. Ha! That would be rich.

I make a cup of tea, not bothering to offer Pierre one as I can't face the cool rejection that I'm sure the offer will elicit. I take it outside to sit on the step in the late afternoon sunshine, to try and clear my head.

Eventually Pierre comes down the stairs, packing tools and his rolled up green overalls into his rucksack as he goes, evidently in a hurry to get out of my house and away as quickly as possible. I get up from the step, still clutching my mug.

"It's finished?" I ask.

"*Oui*," he replies with a curt nod. He pulls on his leather jacket and shrugs the rucksack onto his back, then flings one leg over the motorbike. Just as he's about to fit the helmet over his unruly curls, he pauses and looks at me standing awkwardly by the step.

There's a pregnant silence. And then he speaks.

"It was an honest mistake," he says. "Cédric's really fallen for you. That's why he risked asking, in spite of what everyone has been saying about your situation. He thought it was just gossip."

There's another silence as I try to digest what he's just said. Blimey, even his own brother is encouraging a little adultery on the side now. And then I think, you what? Am I missing something in translation?

"Excuse me?" I say coolly, "what's *my* situation got to do with it? It's his own situation that's the problem. I know you French are very broad-minded about these things but, bourgeois as it may seem, I'm not prepared to get involved with a married man."

There's another silence as Pierre appears to be struggling to understand what I've just said.

"A married man," he repeats, stupidly.

Now he seems to be on the back foot, but I'm just starting to get into my stride. "Yes, poor Marie-Louise. I don't care how open a relationship they have, that's up to them, in fact the whole situation is not something that interests me in the slightest."

"Marie-Louise," he repeats. Now he appears to be completely at a loss. Then he says, very calmly and reasonably, as you would to a lunatic who you were trying not to derange any more than was clearly already the case, "The same Marie-Louise who is married to Florian."

"Precisely," I say triumphantly. And then I realise what he's just said. Now it's my turn to repeat what's just been said. "Marie-Louise is married to Florian." I can feel the blood draining from my face.

Pierre looks at me curiously.

"But..." I stammer. "But if Marie-Louise is married to Florian, who is married to Cédric?"

A grin begins to spread across Pierre's face as the *centime* begins to drop. And then his expression changes to one of sadness. "Gina," he says, speaking very slowly and clearly as if to a complete idiot, "Cédric's wife, Isabelle, died three years ago. Breast cancer. He hasn't looked at another woman since. Until you came along, that is. Marie-Louise was Isa's best friend from school days. She and Florian have been happily married for fifteen years, they have three sons." And then he says more gently, "How can you have lived here all these months and know nothing of this?"

How indeed? I hardly know myself. I suppose it's because I've been so immersed in trying to fathom my own family's complicated relationships that I've effectively shut myself away from the world.

"But she danced with him at Bastille Night," I say lamely, struggling to make sense of everything I've just been told.

"That's because Florian has two left feet, and Cédric loves to dance," says Pierre with a shrug.

"But Nathalie... and Luc..." I tail off, lamely.

"Yeah, it's been tough for them, but Marie-Louise collects them from school some days and others the school bus drops them at my mother's," he nods in the direction of Mireille's house, "so it's not a problem. That's what families are for, after all."

229

There's another silence while I contemplate this, and then think of my own family which seems far too sparse and somewhat lacking in comparison. And then, replaying the conversation we've just had, another thought occurs to me.

"Hang on a second," I say indignantly, "just what are people saying about my situation?"

"Well, first of all you were with that terrible guy, the Anglo-Saxon with the red face. Everyone saw you dancing with him at Bastille Night."

"I was *never* with him," I cry.

"OK, maybe, but then Christine Cortini told Marie-Louise that she and Robert saw you and your English friend being very affectionate indeed on the bridge in Sainte Foy after an intimate meal *à deux*."

I look blank. "My English friend." I'm now the one back in repetition mode.

"Yes, you know, the one with the magnificent breasts. What was her name? Annie."

Oh god. So first Cédric thought I was an item with Nigel Yates and then he thought I was a lesbian. I have a sudden flashback to the scene on the terrace with a scantily clad Annie doing her orgasm impression. Come to think of it, that probably didn't help matters much either.

And then I realise that, despite all this, Cédric still liked me enough to cling on to the hope that he might still be in with a chance. And he finally plucked up the courage to ask me out. I hear my shrill tirade from yesterday echoing in my head, berating him for being a cheating bastard.

Pierre continues, with a nod at the mug in my hand, "He even drank your horrible tea every day, just so he could have a chance to talk to you."

"Oh no, Pierre, I think I've made the most terrible mistake," I wail.

But he's not really listening as he's taken out his mobile phone and is busy composing a text message. He obviously has more important things to deal with, like his own social life for instance, than this crazy English woman who hasn't a clue what's going on in the world beyond her front gate.

With a final irritatingly dismissive shrug and a wave, he clamps the helmet firmly on his head and roars off down the drive and I'm left standing forlornly in the courtyard gazing after him.

Stunned, I sit back down on the step, cradling my head in my hands as I try to absorb all I've just heard. How could I have been so wrong? I feel more of an outsider than ever, as I contemplate the intricate, tightly-knit web of support that is the Thibault family. I've been living in a community that has observed and commented on my every move while I've carried on blissfully unaware. I've been so wrapped up in my own affairs that I haven't made any attempt to find out more about my own neighbours, to understand them, to know their battles and their triumphs, to take part. And worst of all, I've now hurt and insulted one of the best men

I've ever met, who has already suffered more than his share of loss and grief. I've blown my chances with the man of my dreams.

A few minutes later a car swishes by at the end of the drive and I glance up in time to catch a fleeting glimpse of a familiar dark blue pickup. For a second my heart lurches as I think it's going to turn into the drive, but to my dismay it carries on along the lane. Cédric must be going to collect Nathalie and Luc from Mireille's.

I leap to my feet. I have to put this right. I'll go over and ask him to step outside so I can apologise, try to explain.

I hurry up the drive, anxious to get this over and done with, trying to think of the French for "sorry I'm such a complete bloody idiot" and "do you think you can ever find it in your heart to forgive me?" And then I see that a figure in dusty green overalls is coming towards me along the lane, hurrying just as much as I am.

As he draws near, I see the look on his face and I realise that, for once, Pierre's main priority wasn't sorting out his social life. He was texting his brother.

And now no apology is needed. In fact, no words are needed at all as Cédric takes me in his arms and kisses away the tears that are pouring down my cheeks. Then, over the sound of the pounding of my heart, I hear the hoarse, ratcheting cry of a magpie and another's triumphant answering call in the branches of the trees above our heads. And I know that I've come home.

*

Time passes – it could be five minutes, it could be fifty – and suddenly Cédric looks up, distracted by the sight of a small figure dancing along the lane toward us. I turn, still held in the circle of his arms, to see Nathalie. As she draws nearer she calls, "Papa, Grand'mère wants to know if you're going to ask Gina to come and have supper with us?"

Cédric looks down at me, his eyes tender, smiling, the threads of ancient pain and grief still just visible there, but overlain by so many other strands that make up his life, the fabric of which I'm only just starting to understand. "It's not quite the romantic evening *à deux* that I had planned for our first date," he laughs.

I stoop down to hug Nathalie and brush back a strand of her dark hair from her eyes. Looking up at Cédric, I smile back. "I can't think of anything more perfect," I reply.

Nathalie takes hold of the hand that Cédric isn't holding and leads the two of us back up the lane to the little house in the plum orchard. Where Mireille, grinning broadly, already has an extra place set at the table.

Chapter 15.

"Well," says my mother, settling herself at the table on the terrace. "It's certainly been quite a year. Hard to believe that twelve months ago we were here for Liz's funeral. And now here I am again for my daughter's wedding."

She starts taking things out of a Peter Jones carrier bag that she's put on the table before us.

"Here's the hair-band, and I managed to find these rosebuds in silk – pink as directed. I thought it might look pretty with a few of these cream ones sewn on too. I also bought needles and thread as I expect it's highly unlikely that either my daughter or my sister would have such mundane items about the house..." She rummages in the bag.

"And I got this for you. Although I know you'll probably only use it once, living as you do in the depths of the country, but I couldn't resist. Thought it might be useful for tomorrow." She passes me a smaller carrier bag with Harvey Nichols emblazoned on the side and I pull out a beautiful cream leather clutch bag.

"Oh Mum, it's gorgeous," I cry.

"Well I thought it would go with that old top of Liz's you're insisting on wearing. You've got to have something new, after all. It's Yves Saint Laurent – had to be a French designer, of course!"

I hug her hard. "Thank you," I say, suddenly choked with emotion.

She pats my hand and then pulls away. "So glad you like it darling. But you know me and handbags – my absolute favourite thing to shop for."

"Now," she continues, "tell me how you want these flowers on Nathalie's hair-band and I'll sew them on for you."

She sets to, neatly stitching the little silk roses onto the pink band. I can't resist taking the handbag out of its wrapping once again to stroke the fine, soft leather.

"Remind me again," says Mum, "what the program is for this afternoon."

"We have to be at the Notary's office at four thirty for the official bit," I reply. "So there should be time for Luc and Nathalie to come back from school first and change. We'll probably be home again by half-past five, it won't take long."

"And that's just you two, the children and Mireille and me?"

"Yes, the legal bit isn't going to be the slightest bit romantic. That's why we wanted to have the service of blessing in the chapel tomorrow and the party afterwards, for a proper celebration. Tonight Mireille's doing supper at her house – just for the family. Though even so, there're going to be nearly twenty of us, with the brothers and their wives and all the cousins. "

"And then tomorrow sounds lovely. It's very kind of these friends of yours to host the party at their chateau."

"I know, but it's not that grand," I warn her. "The Cortinis are setting up tables in the *chai* for the dinner. It's going to look lovely though. Marie-Louise and Christine are decorating it. And Luc let slip that the brothers are planning some sort of surprise that he's going be helping with – I suspect from his excitement that it may be fireworks for later on."

There's a silence as my mother stitches away and then finally picks up a pair of scissors to snip the thread. She holds up the band.

"How's that?"

"Perfect," I reply. "Nathalie will be delighted. She's insisting on wearing her new dress to the lawyer's office today as well as the party tomorrow. Determined to get her money's worth! Luc's much cheaper to run. All he wanted for the big day was a new pair of trainers."

"Well it's going to be wonderful Gina. And very apt, you having your wedding in a winery. You father would have been tickled pink. As pink as this hair-band in fact." She smiles, then pauses and pats my hand. "I'm just sorry he won't be here to walk you up the aisle. He'd have approved thoroughly of Cédric, you know. And been so proud of how well you're doing with the Master's qualification," she adds.

"Well I've still got to get through the exams in the summer," I say. "And then write my dissertation next year. But I'm really enjoying it. I'm going to try writing a couple of pieces and submitting them to *Carafe* magazine. You never know, maybe I'll end up following in Dad's footsteps after all."

There's another pause, as I wonder whether I can ask the next question I want to put to my mother. I swallow nervously and then say as nonchalantly as possible, "Did Dad ever used to come and stay here? When he was over on his wine-tasting trips, I mean."

Mum considers my question for a moment, apparently concentrating hard on tucking her needle back into its little folder. Then she lifts her head and gives me a searching look, still saying nothing. The silence begins to grow heavy with unspoken meaning and I drop my eyes. I pick up a cream silk rosebud and fiddle with it nervously.

Finally she speaks.

"He loved her, you know," she says very quietly. "I did wonder whether you had realised." There's another pause and I say nothing, my heart beating hard as I digest what she's just said.

"We'd only been married a few months," she continues, "and David had to come to Bordeaux for some wine-tasting event. He hadn't met Liz before – she'd been working in New York for a year, but she'd come back to France, to this house, for a holiday between assignments. So I said 'you two

must meet up since you're going to be so nearby'."
She gives a short, unhappy laugh.

"I knew the minute he got back something had happened. He told me he hadn't had a chance to come here, that work had kept him in Bordeaux. Only I'd already heard from Celia Everett that they'd had him and Liz to dinner while he was staying – she'd chattered on about how lovely it'd been to meet him and how well they'd all got on. Then he said he had something important to tell me. And I said 'that's a coincidence because I've got something to tell you too'. Because I was pregnant with you. And I decided then and there that I wasn't going to let my baby be born into a family that had been ripped apart by this impossible situation. So anyway, he said 'you go first then' – always the gentleman," she smiles. "I'll never forget the look on his face, a terrible mixture of joy and pain. He decided to do the right thing, of course, and stay." Her voice grows stronger as she talks and I realise that perhaps it's a relief for her to be able to share the burden that she's carried alone for so many years.

She reaches across to me. "It's really important that you know, Gina, that he never regretted that decision. Being a father to you. And a good husband to me."

"So that's why you never wanted to come here," I say, holding tight to her hand.

She shrugs. "It was hard, living with the knowledge that I was keeping apart the two people who'd been dearest to me. And neither of them ever mentioned it again, but it was always there, the elephant in the middle of the room. To answer your earlier question, I don't know whether David ever came here when he was over for work. I didn't want to know. Some stones are better left unturned. I knew that whatever happened he would always come home to the daughter he adored. And I knew, too, that Liz would never do anything to hurt you. Or me either, come to that. She was a wonderful sister really and whatever happened between them must have been born of a moment of madness, some irresistible force of nature that was stronger than them both. I felt guilty in a way, for being what got in the way of their being together. I also had to live with the knowledge that they stayed apart for my sake, as well as yours. It's not easy living a life of indebtedness, having to be grateful all the time, you know." She smiles and then reaches over to hug me. I hug her back, hard.

Because only now do I realise how very much I have been loved by my father and my aunt. But most of all by my mother, who was prepared to risk losing her beloved sister for the sake of her unborn child.

There are a thousand more questions I want to ask, but I sense that now is not the time. Mum's already given me an awful lot to digest. And anyway, maybe she's right, some stones are better left unturned. Perhaps sometimes it's better just to let the past be.

Mum strokes my hair. "Anyway, they'd both have been so happy for you today. I wish Liz were here to see how you've ended up. Really it's all because of her that you're here and you met Cédric. Funny how life turns out."

Then she continues, in a brisker tone, "Now that we've got all that out in the open, there's something else I wanted to ask you about. Liz's ashes. Have you already scattered them somewhere?"

I shake my head. "No. I wasn't sure what to do with them. They're in the cupboard in the sitting room." Once Cédric and the children moved in, I realised how bizarre it was to have the urn sitting in such a central, prominent position so I'd quietly put it away.

"Well, I don't know what you think about this idea, but I wonder whether it's time now to let them be together. Why don't we scatter them where we did Dad's, beside his bench at the edge of the ridge?"

I look carefully into her face, but her expression is calm, happier and more peaceful than I've seen in years. "Would you really be OK with that?" I ask.

"The way I see it, they couldn't be together in life, so it's right that they should finally be together in death. I still loved both of them very much, you know. Families are complicated things, Gina. I quite like the thought of having them both at the bottom of the garden."

I smile. "I think it's a beautiful idea Mum. I'll bring the urn over when I come in the summer and we can do it then."

"By the way," she says lightly, "in case you're wondering, when it comes to my turn you can scatter me somewhere else. I've already been the gooseberry for a lifetime so there's no need for it to last an eternity."

"Mum," I protest laughingly, "what a conversation to be having on my wedding day! You've got lots of years ahead of you."

"No seriously," she says, her tone still light, belying her words. "It's important to sort these things out in advance."

"OK, OK. Were you thinking of anywhere in particular then?"

"Oh, I don't know. I've always wanted to travel, so maybe pop me into the ocean somewhere. Although," she adds, with a mischievous glint of black humour in her eye, "there is a little bit of me that will wander forever in the handbag department of Harvey Nic's!"

A rap at the kitchen door interrupts this interesting, if somewhat surreal, line of conversation, and a familiar voice calls, "Cooee! Is the bride at home?"

I leap up from my chair to embrace Annie.

"Love the hair!" I say. She's toned down the platinum look with some slightly more subtle golden highlights.

"Glad you like it," she says, patting it with one hand. "Just had it done for my best friend's wedding." She hugs me hard again.

"Would you like some lunch?" I ask. "We're just going to have a sandwich."

"No, that's OK thanks. I shouldn't really be here at all, but I couldn't resist popping in to say hi as I was pretty much passing your door. I'm off out to lunch with Thomas Cortini. Purely business, of course," she says, with a wicked grin that indicates it's probably going to be anything but. "WineLand is going to be stocking some of the Château de la Chapelle wines and I've selflessly volunteered to break the news to him. Given that I just happened to be in the area."

"That's fantastic!" I exclaim. "The Cortinis will be thrilled."

"Right, well, see you tomorrow. Hope all goes well this afternoon. Give my love to Cédric and the children. Bye Mrs Peplow," she calls, with a wave to Mum. She turns back to me. "Now get out there, girl, and marry that gorgeous Frenchman, before I do it myself!"

Epilogue.

It's an early summer's night and the moonlight is streaming in through the skylights in the bedroom ceiling. I rub my eyes, which are gritty with tiredness, and glance over at the clock. Two twenty.

It must be two years now since my insomnia began and I've given up all hope of ever having a full night's sleep again.

I gaze across at my husband, who is fast asleep beside me, worn out at the end of another hard day's work. Downstairs Luc and Nathalie are asleep in their rooms. Luc will have his beloved iPod plugged into his ears, having fallen asleep listening to his latest downloads. He's taken it upon himself to try to educate me, introducing me to the likes of Blink-182 and Bloc Party, although we still dance around the kitchen to Marc Bolan and the Beach Boys when no-one's watching. And I know Lafite will be curled up at the end of Nathalie's bed, watching over her from his favourite spot.

In my arms, our newborn baby son is just dropping off again after his two a.m. feed. Cédric says he's going to grow up to be a famous wine writer, like his English grandfather and his mother. (In my case I'm not sure that one article to date published in *Carafe* qualifies me for fame, although

Mireille still carries a copy around in her handbag and has shown it to everyone from the postman to the Mayor). But I hope he's going to follow in the footsteps of his father and his namesake uncle and be the next stonemason called Pierre. Forming the next band of Thibault Frères, perhaps, along with his brother Luc and some of his cousins.

I ease myself carefully out of bed, still cradling little Pierre in my arms, and gently put him back in his cot. His long dark eyelashes flutter on his cheek but he doesn't wake.

As I stand gazing down at him in the moonlight, I think about families, picturing the serried ranks of photographs in their frames on the dresser in the kitchen. There's a cluster of small photos of Luc and Nathalie; there's a beautiful print of Isabelle hugging her two beloved children, her face glowing before her cruel illness took hold; there's a picture of Cédric and me emerging from the little chapel at Saint André on our wedding day last year, and a large print, taken by Robert Cortini from the catwalk above the wine vats, of a long table bedecked with wisteria and white lilac, at which a hundred people are raising their glasses to the bride and groom.

And tucked at the back are three black and white photos, one of Liz, one of my mother and one of Dad. Of course, it's not <u>the</u> photo of my father. That ended up as a few extra flaky ashes amongst the ones Mum and I scattered, where the garden gives on to the view of the Downs, one breezy June day last year. Mum was none the wiser, and I know that's what Dad and Liz would have wanted.

Only now do I fully appreciate how much these three loved me. More than love itself.

I think of Mum, alone in her house, keeping herself busy with her Bridge and her shopping, the only men in her life these days her good friends Peter Jones and Harvey Nichols.

As I ease myself back into bed, Cédric turns over with a sigh and puts out an arm to pull me to him. "Are you awake?" I whisper.

"Mmmmh", he mumbles drowsily.

An idea occurs to me.

"Does Patrick Cortini play Bridge?" I whisper again.

Cédric opens one eye and smiles at me. "Ah Gina," he whispers back, "I love the crazy things you say." And he falls straight back into a deep sleep once again.

Never mind, I'll ask Marie-Louise and Christine when I see them at the school gates tomorrow, they're sure to know.

I turn over and pull up the duvet. The clock says two thirty-five a.m.

Suddenly the moonlit room is flooded with fluting, liquid birdsong. A nightingale is singing in the oak trees outside.

I hear my father's voice saying to me, "They are the only bird to sing through the night, Gina.

And they only sing while their babies are in the nest. Once they fledge, the parent is silent again. But it's as if, while their children are with them, they can't help but express the joy in their overflowing hearts."

Smiling to myself I close my eyes. And think, I know just how they feel.

Acknowledgements

Thank you to all the people who have helped me with the writing of this book (either knowingly or unwittingly).

Of course all the characters are entirely fictional, but the Thibault brothers' very high standards of expertise and craftsmanship were inspired by our Super Stonemasons, the Feltrin brothers and their team who have worked miracles to help us create our dream home in France. (And there really is a stonemason called Pierre.)

I am very grateful to those brave souls in the winemaking world who let me loose on their vines and in their cellars: Eric Bonneville and his team at Château L'Enclos, Jacqui and Jean-Michel De Robillard, and especially Pierre and Marisol Charlot whose Château des Chapelains in St André-et-Appelles is the inspiration for so much in this book.

Thanks to Robert Barrière and the Confrèrie des Vins de Sainte Foy Bordeaux who have honoured my husband and me by awarding us the title of Chevaliers of the appellation, and to Florent Niautou in the oenology lab at St André-et-Appelles for sharing his passion for winemaking with us.

And finally my love and thanks go to my sister Carin who encouraged me to keep writing in the face of building dust, despair and writer's block. This one's for you.

About the author...

Fiona Valpy lives in France, having moved there from the UK in 2007. She left behind a career in Marketing and Public Relations to explore new avenues and now teaches yoga and writes. Having renovated an old rambling farmhouse with her husband, she has developed new-found skills in cement-mixing and interior decorating, although her preferred pastime is winetasting.

Seven Magpies is her first novel, inspired by the people and the wines of the Bordeaux region.

Lightning Source UK Ltd.
Milton Keynes UK
UKOW031812160112

185480UK00013B/86/P

9 781849 142236